Bonnie J. Cardone

The Bride Wore Black

*A Cinnamon Greene
Adventure Mystery*

Also by Bonnie J. Cardone

Fiction
Cinnamon Greene Adventure Mysteries
The Bride Wore Black
Murder Dives the Bahamas
Murder Dives the Caribbean

Short Stories
Murder at the Marietta Inn, *Gone Coastal* anthology
The Last of the Recycled Cycads, *Last Exit to Murder*
anthology

Nonfiction
Shipwrecks of Southern California
Fireside Diver

ISBN: 978-0-9897-165-4-3

Published in the United States of America

Sea Scenes
Santa Maria, CA 93455
www.bonniejcardone.com

Dedication

This book is dedicated to perseverance:
"Perseverance is a great element of success.
If you only knock long enough and loud enough
at the gate,
you are sure to wake up somebody."
Henry Wadsworth Longfellow

THE BRIDE WORE BLACK

Chapter 1

It would be, Jilted Lover knew, the wedding of which bride's dreams are made. Cat would be stunning, her black silk gown complementing her black hair and green eyes. Chip, her wimpy groom, wouldn't be able to take his eyes off her.

He wouldn't be the only one. Everyone would be watching the bride. Tears formed in the corners of Jilted Lover's eyes. No one would ever know how Jilted Lover felt. While appearing serene on the outside, Jilted Lover was seething with hate on the inside. But the magical time would come and revenge, "a dish best served cold," would be had.

Imagining the bridal couple getting ready to cut the cake, Jilted Lover smiled.

The bride would take hold of the silver knife. Her groom would put his hand over hers (Jilted Lover shuddered at the thought of them touching). Together, they would cut a slice from the top layer of the cake. The groom would carefully feed his bride a small bite. He would know better than to mash the cake on her face. No one would dare do that. Not to Cat.

The next slice of cake would be for the groom. The bride wouldn't be as careful as he had been and the crowd would laugh at the mess the cake made around his mouth.

After the cake cutting ceremony, the band would begin to play and the bride's father would lead her out on the floor. All eyes would be on them as they danced. *The bride, well aware everyone was looking at her, would smile up at her father as he twirled her expertly around the floor, something most of those present had watched him do at past events.*

After a couple of minutes, Cat's father would hand her off to her new husband. But the couple wouldn't dance for long. The bride would begin to itch as the allergic reaction set in and, as her horrified groom watched, she would collapse in a black silk heap on the floor.

The bride's mother would scream. The shocked guests would rush forward, trying to find out what had happened.

Jilted Lover wouldn't be at the reception and wouldn't be joining the crowd around the bride. Jilted Lover already knew how and why the bride had died.

Chapter 2

I headed northwest to Cliffview on a bright and warm October morning. Dry Santa Ana winds were blowing in from the desert, bringing warm air and chasing the smog out to sea. It didn't make leaving Los Angeles, already difficult, any easier. It's depressing to be in your 30s and fleeing what everyone thought was a successful marriage and career to return to your childhood home and a job with your father. At this point, however, it was all I could manage.

Before I left, I visited the Hollywood house one last time. As it turned out, there wasn't anything to put in storage. Since we wanted to look successful, Ted and I had been renting the superficially beautiful but sparsely furnished fixer upper high in the hills. We also rented a studio in Hollywood and leased the car Ted drove. We only actually owned the eight-year old van I drove (a wedding present from Dad) and several thousand dollars' worth of studio equipment. Ted told me to take what I wanted. After making sure he wouldn't be there, I had stopped at the studio first, choosing a couple of camera bodies, several lenses and two of the newer camera-top strobes.

Ted had also agreed that half of the money in our checking and savings accounts was mine. That wasn't much and it wouldn't last long. I was lucky I had a job, even if it was with my father.

At the house, I packed what remained of my

clothes and personal belongings. Willow's presence was evident everywhere, a constant reminder of Ted's betrayals. She had already replaced me in the bedroom. Soon Ted probably wouldn't even remember my name.

It took much less time than I expected to stow everything I owned in the van. Before I drove off, I took one sad, last look at our house, perched on stilts on the side of the hill. Good-bye house, I thought. Good-bye, unfaithful husband.

I wound my way down the hill in the van and, reaching the bottom, turned right on Sunset Boulevard.

Soon the Sunset Strip disappeared in my rearview mirror and I was driving through Beverly Hills, among massive mansions with well-manicured lawns. In the past, every time I motored along this twisting street lined with tall, graceful eucalyptus trees, I had imagined I was on my way home. I had even picked out the place Ted and I would buy when he was a famous photographer, shooting covers for Vogue and Rolling Stone.

When I reached the on-ramp for the northbound 405 I made a split second decision to stay on Sunset all the way to the beach, then head north to Cliffview on the Pacific Coast Highway. It was a beautiful day and the drive along the ocean would be much more pleasant than that on the Ventura Freeway.

My vintage collection of country music CDs was in a box on the floor. Ted hated country, so the van was the only place I played them. At the next red light, I reached down and picked up the box, putting it on the passenger seat. I selected a Judds disc and slipped it into the CD player. In the past, I'd found it impossible to be depressed when I was listening to Wynonna and her lively mother. Indeed, I was soon singing along with the duo and tapping my left foot. I almost stopped the car in Pacific Palisades and danced on the street when they started singing "Girls Night Out." I love that song.

When Sunset ended at PCH I turned right, then rolled the van's windows down. When the Judds album ended, I chose a new one without even looking. It turned out to be a George Strait. He accompanied me through most of Malibu, almost to Point Dume. Then it was Garth Brooks' turn. His rousing rendition of "Rodeo" made me feel very much alive. The farther north I drove, the better I felt. I breathed in deeply, savoring the ocean's unique smell. The air was warm and the sky was blue, with just a hint of brown (smog) at the horizon. Sunlight danced across the Pacific Ocean. It was just me and Garth in my van, going home. And, for the first time, I began to think that maybe, just maybe, I'd be okay.

Chapter 3

The break-up with my celebrity photographer husband was precipitated by his appearance on The Tonight Show with an up and coming super model he was sleeping with. It was an excruciatingly painful public humiliation. I had excused his infidelities in the past, believing all geniuses are flawed. This time, however, he had gone too far.

I would have left him that night except we were involved in an unfortunate altercation involving his best friend and some stolen king sago palms, during which I accidentally ran over Ted with my van. Talk about guilt! I felt terrible about that and instead of fleeing to my hometown, I added "nurse" to my duties as wife, assistant, office manager and domestic servant while Ted's broken nose and various other injuries healed.

We had been together for eight years. We met as freshmen at Santa Barbara's Windgate Institute of Photography. He was the college's most charismatic and talented student (not to mention good looking) and everyone knew he was going to be famous.

I, on the other hand, had worked for my dad growing up and would probably work for him when I graduated. He owns Greene's One Stop Camera and Photo Shop in the small California coastal town of Cliffview, just ten minutes south of Windgate. Many of the store's customers are institute students.

Dad didn't raise a complete idiot. I knew Ted

would never be interested in me. Instead of joining the adoring groupies who surrounded him, I admired him from afar while I focused on my studies and worked part-time for Dad. My good grades, however, had an unexpected result. When we ended up in a class together, Ted invited me out for coffee and, taking one of my hands in his, uttered five enticing words: "Cinnamon, I need your help."

Turns out, he was close to failing a couple of classes on the business side of photography. Because of me, he graduated. We married four years after we met, just before moving to Hollywood and setting up Quiero Studios with money Dad loaned us.

Ted was the creative side of the business, I did everything else. I had lots of jobs because we had mountains of debt and couldn't afford to hire anyone. While we both believed Ted was on his way up the ladder of success, he wasn't there yet.

Life in Hollywood was exhilarating. We went to nightclubs and met famous people. I enjoyed basking in the reflected glow of Ted's growing celebrity. The flies in the ointment were his propensities to spend money we didn't have and sleep with women he photographed.

True to form, Ted resumed cheating on me as soon as his face was back to normal.

I was microwaving my dinner one evening when my best friend from junior high called. Jeannie got right to the point.

"Have you seen today's LA Times?"

"Haven't had time."

"Well go get the paper, sweetie, and turn to section H, page 12. And Cinnamon, be sure to sit down first."

With mounting apprehension I did as she directed and there, in full color, was a photo of Ted and Willow smiling at the camera with their arms around each other at a famous actor's birthday party. Part of me had known he hadn't reformed. The proof, however, was hard to take.

"Cinnamon. Now are you ready to dump that jerk?"

"I need time to think, Jeannie."

"Why? What are you waiting for? Where's your self-respect? He's never going to change. Wake up, Cinnamon.

"Pack a few things, sweetie, and get your butt over here. You can stay with us while you plan a future without Ted."

After we hung up, I sat absolutely still for a few minutes. Then I stood and walked over to the wall-to-ceiling windows in our home high in the Hollywood Hills. Below me, the bright lights of LA sparkled in a crisp, remarkably clear evening.

What did I have to lose by leaving? Ted might miss me if I were gone. If he was properly contrite and promised to change his ways, I could go back to him. If he wasn't, well, I had absolutely no doubt Jeannie would push me down a path that led to life without him.

I don't have all that much "stuff" and it didn't take long to fill a suitcase. Twenty minutes later I was parking my car in front of Jeannie's neat and tidy yellow stucco house in West L.A. Jeannie and her husband Dave, an architect, had been married ten years and were the ecstatic parents of six-month-old

Alexa. They were the happiest couple I knew. They loved each other and were thrilled with their daughter, conceived after eight years of trying and the spending of thousands of dollars for various procedures. I retrieved my suitcase from my van and walked up to the front door. Jeannie opened it and gave me a badly needed hug. I dissolved in tears.

Jeannie took my suitcase, put an arm around my shoulders and led me into the den, where a small desk lamp cast a soft light. The room looked cozy, comfortable and safe.

Jeannie didn't say anything for a while, she just held me until I finished crying. When the tears dried up, I was exhausted.

"Go to sleep now, sweetie. We'll talk in the morning."

Fresh towels and a washcloth were set out for me in the bathroom. Jeannie had left me a nightshirt, too. When I saw it, I realized I'd forgotten to pack mine. I went to bed, falling into a troubled sleep.

Chapter 4

I spent more than two months with Jeannie, Dave and Alexa. The first six weeks were hell. I lost ten pounds and cried myself to sleep almost every night. Though I wanted to die I lived on. During that time I would have gone back to Ted in an instant if he'd called, which he didn't. He knew where I was because his new studio manager, hired two days after I left, called me numerous times to ask questions, as did his new photographic assistant, hired three days after I left. That they called and Ted didn't incensed Jeannie. She took away my cell phone so I couldn't call Ted in a weak moment, of which there were many. Since Ted never personally sent or answered e-mails, I was allowed to keep my laptop.

Jeannie and I had known each other for more than two decades. We'd become instant friends just after her family moved to Cliffview when we were 11. We were both skinny and small for our age. It was our psyches that bound us together, though. We often wondered what our relationship had been in a previous life or two and were convinced we were old soulmates.

We did have differences. Jeannie planned her life, mine just sort of happened. She had a sweet, happy baby. Her husband was not movie star handsome, nor would he ever be famous. But his face lit up when he looked at his wife and child. Jeannie's life was orderly and busy, mine was freeform and exciting. Compared to hers, however, it seemed considerably less rewarding.

As the weeks passed, the pain of being Tedless diminished. I began to see how hard I had worked and how little I had benefited. Even though I realized it was time to move on, after all those years of focusing on making Ted successful, I had no idea what to do with my own life.

During this directionless phase Dad called. After my mom died in a car accident when I was eight, he raised me and, until my marriage, we were very close. I'd talked to him nearly every day after I'd left Ted. (His first comment about that was "Good for you." It was an echo of a sentiment most people expressed.)

Dad (everyone but me called him "Red" because his hair had been red before it turned gray) said one of his employees had just quit and offered a suggestion: "Why don't you work for me for awhile, Cinnamon? You need a change of scene and I could use some help. Cat Callahan is getting married in a few weeks."

The wedding was a big deal. Cat was the only child of the town's mayor and her wedding would be the social event of the year in Cliffview. It also meant the pressure was on; the videos and photos Greene's One Stop Camera and Photo Shop produced would be posted on the social media and be displayed in the store so they had to be excellent.

Jeannie urged me to accept the offer. "Cliffview is the perfect place for you right now," she said. "You've been taking care of Ted all these years and ignoring your own needs. If you go there you'll have time for you, to figure out what you want.

"Besides, it ought to be an interesting wedding, if it happens that is. Cat was a runaway bride last time, leaving her husband-to-be standing at the altar, remember?"

"Oh yeah," I said. "Jason Satana."

"The one and only. It was the talk of the town for weeks. While Cat's unpopular, Jason is hated. Everyone was thrilled that he got dumped." Jeannie always had the latest Cliffview gossip because her sister lived there. Jeannie's advice made sense; I could use a no-stress, no-pressure interlude to examine my life while I figured out a new, Tedless direction for it.

Dad and I talked and e-mailed several times over the next couple of weeks. "You can have your old room in the house," he said, "As you know, it's just the way you left it."

"Although my pride is pretty well shredded, Dad, I still have some left. If I move in with you I won't have any at all. Are you still seeing that real estate lady, Sandy what's-her-name? Maybe she can help me find a condo or something."

I could almost hear him blush. "Sandy and I see a lot of each other," he admitted. "I'll call her right now and ask her to phone you."

Within the hour I was speaking to Sandy. I took her word that I'd love the affordable one bedroom condo she said was available on Third Street. "Stop by the office when you get here, we'll do the paperwork and I'll give you the keys. Or I can give them to Red," she said, "We're together nearly every night."

Ha, I thought. She's already letting me know she

has dibs on Dad.

While I was staying with Jeannie I did what I could to help out, including babysitting while she ran errands or went out to dinner with her patient husband. In the beginning, I wasn't sure I'd be good at caring for an infant and although Jeannie was too polite to say so, I could tell she had her doubts, too. Things went so well, however, that Jeannie and her husband felt comfortable leaving their baby with me while they took a well-deserved vacation (they called at least once every day). While it wasn't the easiest job I've ever had, Alexa rewarded me with coos and smiles and the days flew by.

When I left for Cliffview, Jeannie and I both cried, me because I loved her and Alexa and I'd no longer have daily contact with them, as well as because I was leaving the sanctuary their home had provided and rejoining the real world.

"We're going to miss you," Jeanne said. "You were a huge help. Who knew you'd be so good with babies? You're a natural. I can hardly wait for you to have a couple of your own."

I didn't tell her she'd be waiting in vain because I'd pretty much ruled out having kids. Part time child care is one thing, years of fulltime care is quite another.

Chapter 5

Even though it caused a great deal of pain to read yet another newspaper article on the upcoming nuptials, Jilted Lover devoured the story, wallowing in the details. A voice in Jilted Lover's head keened, "Chip Forester and Cat Callahan should not be getting married, one of them belongs to somebody else."

While reading the article, Jilted Lover made sarcastic comments out loud.

"The bride," the article stated, "will be wearing a one-of-a-kind black silk dress, designed especially for her."

"The dress will be perfect for her funeral," Jilted Lover announced out loud to nobody.

"The new Mr. and Mrs. Chip Forester will honeymoon in Paris."

"Not if I can help it," Jilted Lover smirked.

"After the honeymoon, the couple will return to Cliffview, where they have bought a house in the new Wilmott Ranch Road development."

Jilted Lover snickered. "Isn't it a shame they will never live in the house together?"

"More than 300 guests are expected to attend the wedding of the popular couple," the article concluded.

"All but one of those guests will be horrified when the bride collapses and dies during the

reception," Jilted Lover added. "That one person will dance on her grave"

Chapter 6

Bonnie Raitt was singing "Luck of the Draw" when I pulled off the 101 and onto Cliffview Avenue about noon. There were buildings I'd never seen before on both sides of the street. They hadn't been there the last time Ted and I visited, nearly a year ago.

Dad had told me his store had the best spot in a new mall and I seemed to recall it had something to do with a bell. I drove west and, about half a mile from the 101, I saw an attractive open air strip mall on the north side of the street. It was a two block long structure of cream stucco with red tile along the top edges. Trees had been planted here and there in the parking lot. A carefully maintained border of grass and flowers separated the lot from the sidewalk. The mall had a grocery store on one end and a home improvement store on the other. In between were numerous small specialty stores and restaurants, including the obligatory Starbucks. The center of the mall contained a bell tower, in which hung a mission bell replica. Right under the tower was Greene's, "Your One Stop Photo and Camera Shop." Dad had gotten this prized location because his was the oldest business in the mall. That he was a prominent member of the town council and a former mayor hadn't hurt.

At noon on this Saturday in October the mall was quite busy. It had been busier still the previous weekend when the annual avocado festival was held. Things would quiet down in the winter and spring but ramp up again in summer, when hordes of tourists came to enjoy Cliffview's famous beach.

I admired the storefront before I went in. It occupied a space nearly twice the size of the Greene's that had preceded it. Inside, Dad and two other salespeople were behind the counters; all of them had customers. I opened the door and walked in. Dad looked up, said, "Cinnamon's here," and waved me over to where he stood with an extremely attractive young couple.

"This is Cat Callahan and her fiancé, Chip Forester. I've told them you'll be shooting their wedding video."

"Nice to meet you," I said.

While Cat was beautiful in photos, in person she was exquisite. Almost as tall as Chip, she had black curly hair, green eyes and a flawless complexion. Chip had brown hair, blue eyes and an earnest looking face. They must have just showered; I could smell Chip's aftershave, although it was overpowered by Cat's expensive perfume, one I would wear myself if I could afford it.

"We've heard a lot about you," Chip said.

"And we saw your husband and Willow on The Tonight Show," Cat added. "That must have been a shocker." She looked me up and down before continuing. "But how could Ted resist? Willow is gorgeous." She patted her hair with one hand.

I froze, then darted a look at Dad. He was frowning.

"Uhm, Cat, honey," Chip said hastily. "She

probably doesn't want to talk about that."

"Oh right," Cat said. "Sorry, I'm sure it's a sensitive subject."

She didn't look or sound sorry.

I missed the first few minutes of the chatter that followed, coming out of my daze when Cat next addressed me. "I'd like to have the wedding video start when I'm getting dressed in the Bride's Room. I'll come in wearing jeans with my hair in curlers and become a beautiful bride as the camera watches."

I should not have stooped to her level but the opportunity was irresistible. "Did you buy a new gown or will you be wearing the one from your last almost-wedding?" I asked. "After all, it was barely used."

Dad strangled a chuckle. Chip blanched, no doubt remembering the groom left standing at the altar and wondering if he'd suffer the same fate. Cat's eyes widened and she gasped.

"I'll be wearing a new dress for the most important day of my life," she said stiffly, her eyes shooting bullets. "That one was white. This one will be black. They're as different as night and day." If looks could kill, I'd be flat on the floor.

Chip recovered first. "I think we're finished here, Cat," he said quickly. "I thought we'd go to Jonathan's for lunch. He wants me to redo his landscaping and I'm sure you'll have some good ideas."

Cat didn't speak. She turned and walked out of the store. Chip followed. "Bye," he said just before the door closed behind him.

"I'm sorry, Dad. I shouldn't have said that. Hope

you don't lose the job on my account."

"She deserved it," he said. "The look on her face was priceless. What a hoot. And I wouldn't worry about the job, it's too late for them to book another photographer. Besides, the mayor is a very good friend of mine and he's paying for the wedding."

"Well," I said. "I'll try not to offend any more customers."

A few minutes later, Dad and I went out to lunch at Juanita's, the Mexican restaurant in the mall. As we talked and ate *enchiladas rancheras*, I had a chance to study him. Just less than six feet tall, he's still lean and fit. While the lines on his genial face seemed a little deeper than they'd been the last time I saw him and his formerly red hair was thinner, he was still a very attractive man.

It wasn't his appearance, however, that made him well-liked, it was his easy smile and laidback manner. He rarely got upset and his only fault was a tendency to avoid confrontation. While that infuriated me on some occasions, I had used it to my advantage more than once.

We were nearly finished with our meal when I said, "Looks like you've lost a few pounds. Doesn't that girlfriend of yours cook?"

Dad blushed. "Sandy's an excellent cook. But we joined the new health club and work out together several nights a week." He looked at me anxiously. "She invited us to dinner tonight, is that OK?"

"Sure. I'd like to get to know this woman, see if she's treating you right," I teased him. "Bet she's why you're wearing your hair a little longer. I like it."

Even though he colored, Dad looked pleased. We

left Juanita's and walked leisurely toward the east end of the mall. I recognized one of the stores. "The Bakery moved here, too. I used to love their chocolate croissants. Does Cat's Aunt Veronica still own it?"

"Sure does. She and her daughter, Georgia, still run it. They'll be baking the cake for the wedding. Remember the anniversary layer? We need to get photos and video of the bride and groom with that."

"Oh yeah. That's the top layer, the one with the miniature bride and groom on it. The newlyweds are supposed to store the layer in the freezer and eat it on their first anniversary."

"That's also the layer they cut a slice from during the reception," Dad pointed out. "I've discovered that's unique to Cliffview. Everywhere else that slice comes from the bottom layer of the cake, yet here it's from the top. No one knows why."

"Do they still mash cake all over each other's face the way Ted and I did? I hated that."

"Some do, most don't," Dad told me. "I don't like it either.

"The mall is doing well," he went on. "You've probably noticed the home improvement center and Starbucks. The newest store is Megan's Hair 'n Nail Salon."

"Is that Megan as in Megan Mauvais?"

"Yes. She started out at another salon in town, then opened her own. She persuaded two other stylists to come with her when she left. That caused a lot of bad feelings."

"Jeannie told me about it," I said. "She gets all the good gossip from her sister."

"You know how it is in Cliffview, population

8,000," Dad said. "There's always some sort of tempest in the teapot. However, while Megan's new business seems to be successful, she lost her boyfriend to Cat."

"Chip Forester?"

"The same. Sandy's not a vindictive person but even she got a kick out of that."

It occurred to me then that Dad seemed to mention Sandy in nearly every other sentence. It was "Sandy thinks" this, "Sandy says" that or "we did" this. Dad had quite a few girlfriends after mom died but none had ever gotten really close to him. Looked to me like this one had. Well, as much as I loved Dad, I had longed for a mother when I was younger. Maybe my wishes were about to come true.

We reached my van. As we got in I said, "Where to?"

"It's just two blocks down on the left. Cliffview Realty. Uhm, Cinnamon, there's something I should tell you about Sandy." He sounded nervous.

"I think I already guessed," I said. "You're serious about her, aren't you?"

"Well, yes, I am. We've been talking about getting married. All I want to say, is don't be fooled by first impressions. She may not be what you're expecting."

"Give me credit, Dad. After some of the guys I brought home do you think I could afford to be critical?"

He laughed, but I could tell he still wasn't at ease. "You did give me some scares," he admitted. "What was the name of that guy who looked like a sheepdog and rode a motorcycle?"

"I'm crushed, Dad," I said. "That was Jerry, my own true love for at least six weeks. Is that the office over there?"

I pulled into a parking space on the street and we jaywalked across it to Cliffview Realty. Dad opened the door for me and we went inside. It was a small office, with just six desks. Two were occupied, one by an attractive older woman who was talking on the phone. She looked up, waved and smiled at us. I smiled back. It was the much younger woman sitting at the other desk, however, who got up and walked toward us. She was about my age and very attractive. She had short, shiny blond hair and vivid blue eyes. She wore a white silk blouse and a bright blue suit with a short skirt. We would have been eye to eye if it weren't for the heels on her smart navy pumps.

"Hi sweetie," she said, putting one of her arms around Dad. They kissed each other on the mouth and turned to me. Like a complete idiot, I stood there with my mouth open. This woman couldn't be Sandy, she was young enough to be, well, his daughter.

"Cinnamon, this is Sandy; Sandy, meet Cinnamon," Dad said, his eyes darting between us.

Sandy appraised me with steady blue eyes before she said, "Nice to finally meet you, Cinnamon." She turned to Dad. "You didn't tell her, did you?"

Dad looked at the ground and shook his head. Sandy turned to me. "I advised him to tell you how old I was before we met but I he didn't, did he?"

"No."

Dad glanced back and forth between us anxiously. "Why don't we lead the way to the condo in your car, Sandy? Cinnamon can follow us in her van."

Sandy started toward the office door and Dad hustled after her, reaching it before she did and opening it. I followed Sandy's trim blue bottom through the door. As I passed him, Dad searched my face for a reaction to his girlfriend. I expect I looked as stunned as I felt.

In the van following Sandy's beige Lexus, my thoughts were in turmoil. I didn't expect my laidback, sensible Dad to be dating someone my age. And, he was thinking about marrying her. Holy shit, how could that work?

I didn't have very long to reflect on the situation, however, because the condo Sandy had picked out for me was only about half a mile away. She parked at the curb in front of a multi-story building with blue-gray siding and white trim. I pulled alongside her in the street and opened the passenger side window. Sandy did the same. "Park next to the elevator," she directed, pointing to the underground garage.

By the time I'd parked, walked around to the rear of the van and opened it, Sandy and Dad had joined me.

"As you can see," I said, as we surveyed the two suitcases and several boxes inside, "I don't have very much. Maybe we can each carry something. Oh, except you, Sandy. You probably don't want to get that beautiful suit dirty."

"It's dry cleanable," she said. "Hand me that box, Red."

On the second floor, Sandy juggled her box and a set of keys while unlocking and pushing the door open. One by one, we stepped inside and set our boxes down on the bare wooden floor. We were in a spacious living room, looking toward the kitchen. The place smelled of new paint.

"This unit has just been refurbished, Cinnamon," Sandy said. "It's quite nice and the rent is very reasonable." She turned to look at me. "When will the rest of your things be here?"

"Everything I've got was in the van. I don't have any furniture."

While they processed the information that I had nothing to fill the rooms with, I walked into the kitchen and opened a few of the cupboards. After that, we inspected the bedroom, large walk-in closet and bathroom. My clothes would take up only a fraction of the closet and I had no bed to put in the big, empty room.

"I've got more than enough furniture," Dad said. "You can take anything you want from the house, Cinnamon."

I had been thinking. "I'll bet you still have my sleeping bag and air mattress in the attic, Dad."

"If you put it there, it's still there," he said. "I've never summoned the nerve to clean out the attic."

"Or any other part of the house," I teased him. "This will be a good excuse to get rid of some junk."

"He does have tons of stuff," Sandy agreed, "and I, too, have suggested more than once that he get rid of some of it."

"Damn," I said. "Since I don't even have a coffeemaker I guess I'll be forced to eat breakfast at The Bakery. I love their chocolate croissants."

"They are amazing," Sandy said, rolling her eyes. "I was happy when The Bakery relocated, it used to be right across the street from my office. If they hadn't moved to the mall I'd probably weigh 200 pounds by now. Speaking of eating, did Red tell you about dinner at my place tonight?"

"I did and she said 'yes.' Let's bring up the rest of your stuff, Cinnamon, then we can figure out what you need from the house."

We did just that. Sandy carried her share of the load, heels, expensive suit and all. When we had all my boxes and assorted stuff in the living room she gave Dad a quick kiss good-bye on the lips and left. In spite of helping with the boxes, she looked just as immaculate as she had when I first saw her. I, however, was badly in need of a shower.

"You could use some furniture," Dad said, eyeing the boxes that contained all my worldly goods. "And I'll bet you don't even have any towels."

I sighed and wiped my damp forehead on the sleeve of my T-shirt. "I guess my brain was elsewhere when I was packing. Every time I went to the house I was worried I'd run into Ted. So I spent as little time there as possible. I'll have to buy some towels.

"I don't really need to furnish this whole place, you know. I won't be here much anyway. I do have the most important things, a clock radio and my coffee mug."

"Ah, a mug," Dad mused, "and no way to make coffee. Want to come over to the house now or later?"

"Let's go now. I do want to look for my sleeping bag. Do you still have the card table? I could use that in the dining alcove."

The house I had grown up in was only five minutes from my new condo. I drove us there. As I parked in front of it, I was reminded how much I loved this old Victorian house, with its a wide front porch, gingerbread trim, two cupolas and white siding. Dad was immensely proud of it and his careful maintenance showed. With four bedrooms and two and a half bathrooms the house was big, too big, for just one person.

We walked up to the house in silence. When Dad opened the front door and we went inside, it was just as if I'd never left. The oak floors still sported the Oriental rugs Mom had carefully chosen during a short-lived domestic phase more than 25 years ago. Thanks to the housekeeper who came in once a week, everything was neat and in remarkably good condition. Thanks to Dad never throwing anything away, there was lots of it. We headed for the kitchen, which was just off the dining room that had been converted to a den when I was in high school. Besides the comfortable sofa and two reclining chairs it contained a large screen TV and a high quality stereo system. Built-in bookcases lined the walls and still displayed my high school softball trophies, earned when I was the team's pitcher. I joined Dad in the huge kitchen, modernized about a decade ago.

"Want a Diet Coke?" he asked.

"Sure," I said. I took the can he offered and popped the top open, then took a long sip.

"Well," he said. "What do you think?"

"Of what?" I said, drawing a blank.

"Sandy."

"She seems nice," I fudged noncommittally. "Just how old is she?"

"Her birthday's in March, she's a month younger

than you."

"She's a month younger?" I was incredulous.

"I know, I know. I thought she was too young when I met her, too."

"Where did you meet and how long have you been, uh, seeing her?" I asked, taking another sip of my Coke. Somehow I couldn't use the word "dating."

"She moved here about five years ago. You know how small this town is. I kept seeing this really cute blond at the hardware store, the grocery store, The Bakery and the post office. I was finally introduced to Sandy and her husband at a Chamber of Commerce banquet."

"She's married?"

"Not anymore. She divorced her husband when she found out he was having an affair with Cat Callahan."

"Oh no. Was Sandy married to Jason Satana?"

"Yep. They moved here from LA. They'd only been here a few months when Jason sold Cat a condo. You can guess what happened next. Sandy was devastated when she found out. Cat and Jason got engaged before the divorce was even final."

"Then Cat left him at the altar. Sandy must have loved that," I said.

"She was among the people who felt Jason got what he deserved," Dad said.

"I gather his real estate practices are slightly shady," I said.

"Yeah, that bothered Sandy. He's a wheeler-dealer. She was always afraid he'd do something that would send both of them to prison."

"Jason's still around, isn't he?"

"Oh yeah. Though he lives in Santa Barbara he works here."

"So, how did you and Sandy get together?"

"Well, we got to talking one time and she told me she was a scuba diver. I mentioned the Wednesday Warriors trips on the *California Diver* and invited her to come out on one with me.

"We had great weather on that first trip to Santa Cruz Island, flat seas, sun all day, you know how beautiful it can be out there. Sandy and I made three dives together. She surprised the heck out of me, she's a darn good diver. She's in great shape, too."

"I noticed," I said dryly.

Dad continued his tale as if he hadn't heard me. "The old farts I dive with were green with envy when they met my new buddy." He chuckled and rubbed the palms of his hands together with great glee. "Then, on the way home we were standing on the deck on the bow of the boat as it came into the harbor. Sandy kept looking up at me and finally said, 'Are you ever going to ask me out?' Until then I had no idea she was interested in me.

"So, I took her to dinner in Santa Barbara after the trip. And things just kinda happened after that."

"And you've been seeing her how long?" I asked.

"Nearly a year. She's funny and smart...."

"...and extremely attractive," I finished. I hated the stirrings of jealousy I felt. Dad had always been mine, first, last and foremost. It hadn't occurred to me I'd ever have to share him, especially not with someone my age.

As if reading my mind, Dad went on. "I worried about the age difference at first, but it hasn't been a problem. I certainly know a lot about females your age. I raised you, didn't I?" He smiled and put an arm around my shoulders.

There was no refuting his statement. I'd had a happy, fun childhood. Dad and I had gotten along great with the exception of a few bumps in my teenage years. We had spent a lot of time together until I started college and met Ted.

"Let's go see what you've got in the attic, Dad," I said, changing the subject and finishing my Coke. "If I wait too long, I'll lose my nerve."

"It is pretty crammed," he admitted.

We walked back to the living room and climbed the stairs to the second floor. The four bedrooms and two bathrooms opened off the landing there. Access to the attic was through a large storage room opposite the bedroom that had been mine (in Dad's eyes it still was).

I stood in the doorway of my old room. It looked exactly the way it did when I left Cliffview after graduating from Windgate. Well, not exactly. Since I no longer inhabited it, it was a whole lot neater.

"See anything you want?" Dad asked hopefully.

"I don't think so. You may not have noticed, but I've gotten quite a bit older since I lived here."

Dad opened the storage room door and grabbed a cord that hung from the ceiling. It pulled down a door with a ladder on it. Dad unfolded the ladder and started up with me close behind. At the top, he stopped, flipped a switch and the lights came on. Dad stepped into the attic. When I got there he was surveying the scene with dismay. The large area was crammed with stuff, much more stuff than I remembered. Dust particles danced in the sunlight filtering through the old lace curtains on the windows. It was hot, with that old air smell that comes from being closed up.

I sneezed, agitating the dust particles, which caused me to sneeze again.

"I guess it's been a while since I've been up here," Dad said. "You'll be lucky to find anything in this mess."

"You aren't kidding." I exclaimed, fishing a tissue from my pocket and blowing my nose. I tried to remember the last time I'd been up here and couldn't.

We moved among the piles, looking for something familiar.

"Aha." I said. "My sleeping bag." I moved an old lamp and a dusty suitcase and retrieved the blue drawstring bag. Rolled up right next to it was the deflated air mattress. "*Voilá*," I announced, holding up my treasures triumphantly.

"Beginner's luck," Dad said. "Now let's see you find the card table."

I carried the sleeping bag and mattress to the top of the stairs, then went back and got the little lamp. "I'll need a table to put this on," I said.

"I feel guilty giving you castoffs, honey. Why don't you take some nice things from downstairs?"

"Nonsense, a scavenger hunt is more fun. Find me a table for my lamp," I demanded.

"How about this one?" he asked, holding up a small round table.

"Sold. Oh look, my scuba gear bag. I don't remember bringing that up here."

I unzipped the bag and started pulling equipment

out. "Probably wasn't the best idea in the world to leave my wetsuit folded up in here. Has it only been a year? Now it's permanently creased. Looks like I'll need a new mask, look how yellow the skirt is. Think there's hope for my regulator?"

"The dive store can tell you that," Dad suggested. "Bring the bag downstairs."

"Okay," I said. "And I'm forgetting my mission. I need furniture." I repacked the bag and carted it over to the top of the stairs. By then Dad had located the card table and its four folding chairs. I moved a floor lamp over to the pile and we began carrying everything down three flights of stairs. I chose a couple of pieces of furniture from the living room, then we loaded everything in my van. After we unloaded it at my condo I said, "I think that's going to do it for now. But I'll need dishes, a coffeemaker and towels. Isn't there a discount store nearby?"

"The closest one is in Ventura. I'd try Maria's first if I were you," Dad said. "Her prices are a little higher but you won't have to drive far. She should have everything you need."

"Good idea. It's in the mall now too, isn't it? Want me to drop you off at the store?"

As I drove to the mall Dad kept up a running commentary on what was new in Cliffview. Just before I dropped him off he reminded me we were having dinner at Sandy's. Oh goodie, I was really looking forward to that (not).

Chapter 7

Maria's is a Cliffview institution. Owned by Maria and John Alvarez for 25 years, it had grown from a small, one room shop to an upscale business housed in a two-story building. With a motto of "Fine Things for the Home," Maria's carried linens, dishes, crystal and kitchen ware. Inside, the wooden floors gleamed and everything sparkled. Maria was talking to a customer when I came in, but she greeted me warmly.

"Cinnamon. So good to see you. I heard you were back in town."

Maria's customer turned toward me. She was very attractive. Several inches taller than me, she was slender, with short, professionally tousled dark hair. In shiny, tight black pants and a short-sleeved top with blue, white and black stripes, the woman could have stepped from the pages of a fashion magazine. Quickly but deliberately her glance flicked from my head to my toes. Then her large brown eyes met mine. "I'm Megan Mauvais, owner of Megan's Hair 'n Nail," she said.

While we'd never met before Megan's reputation had preceded her. "I've seen your shop," I said. "When I get settled, maybe I'll come in to see you. Think you can do anything with this?" I indicated my straight auburn hair. I couldn't remember when I'd had it cut last.

Megan eyed my head critically before touching

my hair with two impeccably manicured fingers. "It's an unusual color," she said. "Is it natural?"

The tone of her voice was condescending and, without thinking, I responded in kind. "Yes. It's why my parents named me Cinnamon."

"Oh," Megan said flatly. She was silent for a moment then continued, "What did you have in mind?"

"Oh, I don't know. I'd just like it to look good when I'm working the Callahan wedding."

Megan's eyes widened and she stiffened. "I'd trim it a bit and do a little layering. Here's one of my cards." Her tone held no warmth. She produced a business card from her purse and handed it to me. Then, nodding curtly to Maria and me, she picked up a package and walked away.

Maria and I watched her leave. As she pushed open the door, she looked back and threw me a glance of pure malevolence. When the door closed behind her I said, "Oops," and covered my mouth with one hand. "Guess I shouldn't have mentioned the wedding. I forgot she and Chip were engaged before Cat preempted him."

Maria lifted one eyebrow. "I wouldn't worry about offending Megan," she said. "She's not very popular around town. We call her 'Malicious Megan.'"

I shivered. "If she's so unpopular, how does her business survive?"

"She's a very talented stylist. Few are fond of her but a lot of people like her work. Now, what can I help you with?"

"I have a new, totally unfurnished condo. I need

towels and kitchen stuff right now, maybe some other stuff later."

"Want help finding something?"

"I'll only know what I want when I see it," I said. "I think I'll just browse for awhile."

"Take all the time you need," Maria said. She turned her attention to another customer who had walked up and I went off on my own.

Homemaking has never been my strong suit. I would have felt more at home choosing stuff from the Maria's I knew as a child, the one where everything was in one small room. The primary color in my condo was white. Blue goes well with white, I thought. I chose a set of blue bath towels, then some blue and white kitchen towels. I carried those over to a counter near the register and went upstairs. In a few more minutes I had everything I thought I'd need.

Maria scanned my purchases at the register. "I see you're choosing blue and white, it's a popular color scheme these days. Did you know Cat's having a black and pink wedding? She'll be wearing a black gown, her attendants will be in pink and carry pink roses, and the groom and his men will be in black with pink boutonnières."

"Someone told me that," I said.

"Cat's dress was designed especially for her. I'm sure it cost the mayor a bundle," Maria added.

"I bet."

Maria got ready to total my bill. "Now, what else do you need?"

"That should do it for now," I said. "I think I have enough to get by, at least for now. Now it's on to the grocery store."

Maria and another salesperson helped load my purchases in the van. Then I drove across the mall to the grocery super store.

I spent a lot of money there, too, since I needed everything from toothpaste to dish soap. I'm sure I boosted the local economy.

Once home, it took me several trips to empty the van. After I put everything away, I made coffee using my new coffeemaker and sat drinking it in the rocking chair.

When the coffee was gone, I took a hot shower before dressing in clean jeans and a T-shirt. Just before 6:30, I set off for Sandy's. Her house was only five blocks away, so I walked. Cliffview streets are lined with trees, mostly several varieties of eucalyptus, grown tall and fragrant in the decades since they were planted. While the day had been an exceptionally warm, the sun was setting and the air was cooling rapidly. Most windows and doors would soon be closed and silence would descend. While they were open, however, the sounds of laughter, music, people talking and TV shows drifted out to me as I walked. The streets were busy with cars hurrying hither and yon.

Sandy's house was a small, recently remodeled bungalow, pale green with white trim. A white picket fence surrounded the yard. Borders of colorful flowers lined the walkway leading to the front porch. Window boxes and hanging planters added greenery and more flowers. Dad's bicycle leaned against one wall on the porch and he answered the doorbell.

Chapter 8

"Hi honey," Dad said, opening the screen door. He had recently showered and shaved. He looked and smelled good.

As we walked toward the back of the house he asked me if I was settled.

"I've got a chair, a TV, a coffeemaker and towels in the bathroom," I replied. "Even so, the place is still pretty empty."

Sandy's voice came from the kitchen. "She could probably use a drink, Red."

"That I could," I admitted. Dad led me to the kitchen. The house looked like Sandy. Everything was neat and, well, pretty. Hardwood floors gleamed throughout, covered with expensive looking area rugs. The living room was decorated in shades of pale green and white, with lots of plants. The formal dining room looked absolutely formidable. We ended up in a large, modern kitchen. The white cabinets and pale yellow walls made it look very cheerful and bright. Just off it was a nice sized great room, with a fireplace, a comfortable looking tan sofa and an entertainment center with a large screen TV.

Sandy was putting something in the oven. Dressed in jeans and a black short-sleeved mock turtleneck, she was no less attractive than she had been in the afternoon, only now she seemed a bit more relaxed.

"What's your pleasure, Cinnamon? Beer, wine,

soda?"

"I'll take a beer."

"Great. Red thought you might be interested in microbrews. Check out the fridge, I stocked up."

Beaming, Dad opened the two-door, stainless steel refrigerator. Inside were five different microbrews. I chose a honey wheat, which Dad poured carefully into a chilled mug.

"We're just having steaks, baked potatoes and salad," Sandy said. "You haven't turned vegetarian on us, have you?"

"I don't think I could. I love a good steak."

"Since lobster season is now open, we'll have to plan a lobster dinner," Dad said. "Once we catch some lobster that is.

"Cinnamon used to be pretty good at that. Her largest was eight pounds and she got it when she was only 16." He ruffled my hair and I grinned at him.

"I'm sure Cinnamon does a lot of things better than I do," Sandy said lightly. I thought there was an edge to her voice.

"Bugs taste the same no matter who catches them," Dad said. "And no one cooks them better than the old man."

"You're also the best lobster cleaner, I know," I added. Dad knew I hated cleaning game, especially lobster because they had to be killed first.

"I'll clean all the lobsters anyone gets," Dad announced magnanimously, "as long as I get to eat 'em."

"Hear, hear," I said. "Does this mean I can come on the Wednesday trips, too?"

"I didn't know you still dived," Sandy said.

"Once a year, during my visit here at Thanksgiving. We found my gear in the attic today and remembered how much fun we used to have. Whatever happened to John Carey, Dad? I'll never forget that 13 pound bug he caught at San Nicolas Island. What a monster."

"Was it ever. I ran into John about four years ago. He said he and Joan were into warm water diving and don't 'do' California any more. They were planning a trip to Palau. He certainly was a character. Remember the time he...."

"Excuse me," Sandy interrupted, "the steaks are ready whenever you are, Red."

"I'd better cook them, then." Dad took the platter of raw steaks from Sandy and headed for the sliding doors of the great room. Outside, on the redwood deck, I could see a gas barbecue. Dad pushed the screen open and walked onto the deck. I watched as he carefully arranged three steaks on the grill. He fussed over them for a few minutes before coming back inside.

"Anything else you want me to do?"

"I can help, too," I chimed in.

"Everything's under control," Sandy said. "I just tested the potatoes and they're done. I'll fix the salad next. You had a busy day, Cinnamon. You should just relax. Have a seat." She pointed to the sofa.

I had been standing by the bar that separated the kitchen from the great room. Now I walked over to the sofa and sank down into it. "Wow, is this ever comfortable. Don't let me fall asleep."

"Don't worry," Dad said. "Your snoring would spoil our dinner."

"I don't snore," I protested.

"Of course not," Dad answered, looking heavenward.

"Children, children," Sandy chided us. "No fighting before dinner. And shouldn't you be checking on those steaks?"

"I'll get right on it." Dad headed toward the deck.

Sandy opened a bag of prewashed salad mix and dumped it in a big wooden dish. "Do you think you'll stay in Cliffview?"

"I don't know. My life is kind of on hold. I just knew I couldn't continue being with a man who made a fool of me on national TV."

"We saw that program," Sandy said. "It was worse than what Jason did to me."

"How'd you find out about him and Cat?"

"My mom had cancer and was in hospice care so I went home to be with her. She died while I was there, so I stayed on with my father for a few more weeks. I wasn't able to reach Jason when I was ready to come home and left a message on his voice mail. He didn't get it in time. I walked in on him and Cat in our bed." She sounded bitter.

"I'm sorry, Sandy. That's a tough way to learn about an affair."

Just then Dad stuck his head in the door. "It'll be just another five minutes, girls."

"I'm all set in here," Sandy told him. To me she said. "I was finding it hard to trust men until I met Red."

"He's one in a million," I said.

"I agree. What would you like to drink with dinner, Cinnamon? Another beer? Red, I know, will want water."

The rest of the evening passed quickly. We made small talk as we devoured our meals. Sandy offered strawberries and cantaloupe for dessert and they also disappeared quickly. Afterward, she insisted Dad and I retire to the family room while she loaded the dishwasher. We played double solitaire until she joined us, then we played a couple games of pinochle. Somewhere around 9:30 I stifled a yawn and suddenly realized how tired I was.

"That's going to be all for me, folks," I said. "I'm beat. I'm going home to my sleeping bag."

"Did you drive, Cinnamon?"

"I walked. It's only a few blocks."

"Then I'll escort you home. Cliffview isn't as safe as it was when you were growing up here."

Although I tried to dissuade him, Dad would have none of it. Sandy agreed I shouldn't walk home alone, though as the two of us said our goodbyes, she didn't look very happy.

"Are you coming back?" she asked.

Dad looked embarrassed. "I'll see you tomorrow, Sandy. Thanks for dinner, it was great as usual." He stashed his bike in her garage, gave her a quick kiss and we walked off together.

Cliffview's streets were nearly deserted. Our running shoes made no sound on the sidewalk. The old fashioned street lights cast golden circles ahead of us and eucalyptus trees towered gracefully above us, their foliage still and black. When the sun goes down, the air along the coast cools off quickly. I was glad I'd brought a lightweight jacket. Dad put an arm around my shoulders and I put an arm around his waist.

When I was sure Sandy wouldn't hear us I said, "I hope I'm not spoiling your love life, Dad."

"Don't you worry about that," he said quickly and changed the subject. "Tomorrow you and I need to discuss Cat's wedding. You should also introduce yourself to Pastor Arneson, check out the church sanctuary and reception hall, and talk to Cat and Chip about what they'd like the video to cover. The wedding is only two weeks away."

"I'll bring my video camera and take some test shots. It's been a while since I've worked a wedding."

"Good idea. But I'm sure you'll do fine," Dad said. "Shooting a wedding is like riding a bike, once you know how, you know how forever."

We walked on in silence, enjoying the night. Dad and I hadn't walked with our arms around each other since I was in junior high, when I thought he was the most wonderful man in the whole world. He dropped several spots when I was in high school but had regained his status since. A lump formed in my throat.

"It's good to be home," I said. And when I said it, I realized it was true.

"I'm glad you're back, Cinnamon," Dad said, squeezing my shoulders.

He walked me to my condo and insisted upon coming inside and looking around. Then he went out, closing the door behind him. After I turned the deadbolt I said, "Good night, Dad."

"See you in the morning, honey," came the muffled reply.

By the light of the small lamp in my bedroom, I

changed into a T-shirt and bikini panties. After I washed up, I crawled into my sleeping bag. I slept the sleep of the forgiven and didn't wake until the sun was well above the horizon.

Chapter 9

Although my supplies included coffee, juice and bread for toast, I had no newspaper to read while I ate my breakfast the next morning. Besides, my taste buds longed for a chocolate croissant and I knew where to get one. I dressed quickly, grabbed my sunglasses and headed for The Bakery. It was less than a ten-minute walk. The day was cool and clear. I felt rested and energetic, almost energetic enough to jog.

The Bakery has three tiny tables inside. Through a sliding glass door I could see the little patio with several more tables under red and white striped umbrellas. Heat lamps kept it a comfortable temperature.

Veronica waited on me. A short, plump woman, she had flawless skin, long, graying brown hair gathered in a bun, brown eyes and a perpetually cheerful, friendly nature. Widowed shortly after her only child was born, she had bought The Bakery from its original owner, her boss, when he retired.

"Welcome back, Cinnamon. We heard you were coming home. It's so good to see you." She turned and yelled into the kitchen, "Georgia. Cinnamon's here."

Georgia appeared in the doorway and came over to stand next to Veronica. Both of them seemed genuinely happy to see me. Georgia, who was several years younger than me, had her mother's sunny disposition. She was taller than her mother and, except for her slender figure, looked much the way Veronica had when she was the same age. This could be ascertained by perusing the gallery of family photos hanging on one wall. How Georgia stayed slim while working in The Bakery was a mystery. How she and her mother maintained a close working relationship while living together was another mystery. I thought it was because they were almost like twins, though born in different decades.

"I really need a chocolate croissant," I told them. "No one in LA makes one half as good as yours."

I picked out the croissant of my dreams and asked for a large cup of vanilla bean coffee. Veronica insisted upon making these items a welcome home gift and wouldn't let me pay for them.

"You enjoy them on the house this time, Cinnamon. We know you'll be back for more."

I took my prizes and headed for the patio. The largest table had a pile of newspapers in the center and room for eight. Three people sat around it, all of them reading sections of the Santa Barbara News-Press. This was the "singles table" I remembered from years ago. I sat down and snagged the section with the comics, being careful not to look at anyone. I've never been a morning person and I hate talking to anyone until I've had at least one cup of caffeine.

Luckily, I got through the comics in silence. I had finished my croissant and was in the middle of the lifestyle section when a voice hailed me.

"Cinnamon! Red said you were back in town."

My annoyance faded when I realized the source of the voice was one of Dad's best friends. With him was his long time girlfriend, a woman of his own vintage.

"Paul and Cathy. It's really good to see you."

"Come sit with us, Cinnamon," Paul commanded. "It's been a long time." Just under six feet tall, he had a luxuriant mustache and beard, reminiscent of St. Nick's. He grew facial hair, he told everyone, to make up for the hair that no longer grew on his head. He was about 25 pounds overweight, a fact made obvious by the T-shirt and shorts he wore.

I put down the paper and took my coffee over to their table. I'd known Paul Patterson most of my life. He, Dad and I were all members of the Wednesday Warriors. Paul was the publisher of the Cliffview Chronicle and Cathy Doherty was his society page editor. About my height, she weighed a great deal more. Her best features were her short, brown hair, now mostly gray, and her lively personality. While Cathy and Paul had been dating for so many years no one remembered seeing either of them with anybody else, they maintained separate living quarters and seemed in no hurry to tie the knot.

Paul waited until I set my cup down before giving me a quick hug. Cathy followed suit.

"You look great Cinnamon," Paul said. "I hear you've rented a condo on Third. Think you're back for good?"

"I don't know. I need to figure out what I want to be when I grow up and this is as good a place as any to do it."

"Well, your dad is thrilled."

Before we a chance to say anything more, a man stopped at our table. He was tall, with black, almost kinky hair and a prominent nose. After "Good morning," he said: "Hey Cinnamon, I'm Jason Satana. I hear you've rented a condo in town. If you're ever in the market to buy some property, give me a call. I have listings a lot of the other agents don't." He handed me a card, winked at me and walked away. The tall, attractive dark haired woman with him glanced curiously at me before following him. As they went through the door to The Bakery, she grabbed hold of his arm and threw me a "he's taken" look.

"He doesn't lack for nerve, does he?" Cathy said in a low voice. "He knows his ex-wife is dating your dad and that she arranged your condo rental. Yet here he is, trying to get your business."

"What a jerk," I said.

"I wouldn't buy anything from him, not even a Girl Scout cookie," Paul said.

"The townspeople loved it when Cat left him at the altar. We all felt he got what he deserved for cheating on Sandy. She's a really nice gal." Cathy turned to me. "Have you met her yet?"

"I had dinner at her house last night," I said.

"She's a good cook and she makes Red very happy," Paul said. "I like her a lot even though he dives with her now instead of me. He was the best dive buddy I ever had."

"How come no one has ever been able to catch Jason in some shady deal and put him out of business?" I asked, hoping to change the subject. Talking about Sandy made me uneasy.

"He never seems to do anything illegal, although some of his practices are questionable," Paul said.

—

"Sounds like he and Megan Mauvais would make a nice couple," I said. "She's another business stealer from what I've heard."

"They did date for a time and even bought his and hers BMWs. His is black, hers is blue. They broke up shortly thereafter and now they can't stand each other," Cathy said. "I think they're too much alike."

"I don't suppose I'll see him at Cat's wedding," I said.

"He wasn't invited," Cathy said. "And though he tries to act as if getting left at the altar on his wedding day was no big thing it must have been a huge blow to his monumental ego."

"I'll bet he was livid," I said.

"It was wonderful to watch," Cathy said, launching into a description of what had happened in vivid detail. She finished by saying, "The reception had already been paid for so they held it anyway. It was the only non-wedding wedding reception I've ever been to. Even though they footed the bill, the mayor and his wife seemed to be having a great time. I don't think they liked Jason very much either."

"Jason will never forgive Cat," I said.

"And you know he's just dying to get even," Paul added. "Both Cat and her parents are afraid he'll do something to ruin her upcoming wedding."

"Surely he wouldn't hurt her."

"No," Paul said. "They are worried, however, that he might do something to embarrass her."

"Speaking of weddings," I said, glancing at my watch. "I better get moving. I've got things to do today."

I said goodbye to Paul and Cathy and left The Bakery.

The mall was beginning to fill with cars and people. At Greene's One Stop Camera and Photo Shop, Dad was glad to see me. "Cinnamon, I was just about ready to run over to your condo and make sure you were up. You haven't answered any of my calls."

"Guess I better get used to leaving my cell phone on all the time again," I said, taking it out of my purse.

"Cat called this morning," Dad said. "Chip can't get away from the nursery, so you'll be meeting with her only. She said to call before you come over. Here's her number." He handed me a slip of paper with a telephone number on it, then turned his attention to one of several people waiting at the counter.

In his office, I sat down at his desk. I noticed that in addition to several pictures of me there was now a prominent one of Sandy. Damn. My head knew it was good he had a woman in his life, but why did it make me feel so left out?

I punched in the number Dad had given me and Cat answered on the second ring. She lived south of Cliffview Avenue, in a complex fronting Cliffview Park and just beyond it, the beach.

It took me just five minutes to drive there. Her apartment was in a well-maintained two-story beige stucco structure. The ground level units had patios with grapestake/latticework fences. The second story units featured balconies. The apartments probably rented for twice what mine did because they had an ocean view. Since it was October, I was able to find a

—

49

parking space just two blocks away. Closer parking was restricted to those with permits and, in the summer during the day, those without would have to pay to park in a lot even farther away. Cliffview's famous beaches and shallow, sheltered bay were immensely popular then.

I found the entrance to Cat's second floor condo and went up the steps. She answered the door when I knocked. Once again, I was struck by her incredible beauty, something she was well aware of. Today her dark hair was pulled back in a ponytail and she wore a green silk T-shirt that matched her eyes. Tucked into white shorts, it showed off a slender yet curvaceous figure. Her long legs were lightly tanned, her white leather sandals displayed freshly manicured nails.

She greeted me coolly. "Good morning, Cinnamon, come on in." She led me into the living room. The condo was beautifully decorated, with Kelly green the dominant color. The furniture was expensive. I would bet her parents helped decorate it with the liberal use of their credit cards.

An attractive woman about my dad's age stood in the doorway to the kitchen. She wore white slacks and a pink silk blouse, which complemented her well coiffed silver hair. I knew who she was because I'd seen her photo in the Cliffview Chronicle issues Dad started sending me when I moved to LA. We'd never met, however, because the Callahans had moved to Cliffview after I'd left.

"Mother," Cat continued, "this is Cinnamon Greene, Cinnamon, this is my mother, Margo."

Margo walked over to me and I extended my

hand. She took it with all the warmth of a cold fish.

"Nice to meet you," I said, using the super polite tone I had developed to deal with the models Ted was always introducing me to.

"Come sit down," Margo said, indicating the sofa. There was a large mirror behind it on the wall and, as I turned to sit down, I saw Margo admiring her reflection in it. She patted a nonexistent stray hair into place and leisurely turned her head from side to side before turning her attention to me. "Your dad is so thrilled you're back," she said. "He has sung your praises so profusely we are expecting a wedding video extraordinaire."

"Sometimes Dad gets a little carried away. I wouldn't expect the video to win any Academy Awards," I replied.

I took a pad and pen out of my purse as Cat sank into a chair opposite me. When I looked up, she was admiring herself in the mirror. In a gesture that duplicated the one her mother had just made, she patted a nonexistent hair into place and turned her head slightly from side to side, looking for some imperfection. Apparently not finding any, she reluctantly removed her gaze from her own image and fixed it on me.

"Your place is beautiful," I said. "Green is most certainly your color."

She smiled and looked pleased. "I spent a lot of time choosing the furnishings and had the paint for the walls specially mixed."

Margo sat down on the sofa next to me. "Have you heard the color scheme for the wedding will be black and pink?" she asked.

"The men will be in black and the bridesmaids in pink?"

"Yes. The girls will be wearing pink silk dresses and carrying bouquets of pink roses."

"How many attendants are there?" I asked, making notations on my pad.

"Two flower girls, a ring bearer, four bridesmaids and the maid of honor, Cassidy. She's blonde, the others are brunettes."

"We'll be the most attractive wedding party this town has ever seen," Cat continued immodestly. It was obvious she had no problem with self-esteem.

"How about the groom and his men?"

"What about them?" Cat looked surprised.

"I'm going to film you getting ready. Do you want me to film them, too?"

"Whatever for? Guys getting dressed are boring. Nobody needs to see them until just before they enter the sanctuary."

"And you want the entire ceremony on video as well, right?"

"Yes. Try not to be obtrusive. People will be there to see me and I don't want them distracted. You'll need to be at the rehearsal on Friday so you'll know exactly what's going to happen. Oh, by the way, you and your father are invited to the dinner after the rehearsal."

"What are you planning to wear, Cinnamon?" Margo asked, eyeing my jeans and Greene's polo shirt with distaste. "This is a formal church wedding."

I stifled an impulse to say, "My best sweats," and took a minute to gain control of myself. I answered calmly, "I've got a very nice powder blue silk pantsuit. No one will know I'm just a lowly photographer."

Margo and Cat looked at each other, then at me. "That should be fine," Margo said.

"Is there anything else you want?"

"Be sure to get a close-up of me in my traveling outfit," Cat said. "It's a green silk number that's just beautiful."

I felt a headache forming over my left eye. "Well, I guess that's all I need to know," I said. "I'm going to the church next, where I'll take a few practice shots and talk to the pastor."

I stood up. Margo remained seated, but Cat joined me and, after a quick glance at herself in the mirror, followed me to the door. "Call me if you think of anything else," I said.

Once the door closed behind me, I ran down the steps and jogged to my car. I couldn't get away from that condo fast enough. I had begun to feel very sorry for Chip. He obviously had terrible taste in women, going as he had from Malicious Megan to Callow Cat.

Chapter 10

Cliffview had seven churches, the largest and oldest of which was the nondenominational Church by the Cliffside. I had gone to Sunday school here and been a member of the high school youth group. Church rummage sales, spaghetti dinners and Christmas programs had been the centerpieces of Dad's and my life until I entered college. While he still attended Sunday services, I had developed new interests. The pastor who had shepherded the congregation when I was growing up had retired shortly after I moved to Hollywood. I knew his replacement by name only.

The church had a picture post card setting on a cliff high above the ocean, with the parsonage a bit more inland. They were surrounded by several acres of land, purchased decades before anyone dreamed it would become so valuable. There was a carefully cared for green lawn. Large eucalyptus, silver maple and other trees framed the buildings.

A new sanctuary had been built when I was in college. My photographer's eye thanked those who had insisted its design complement the original buildings.

I left my van in the parking lot and walked to the parsonage. A little girl of about seven, with huge blue eyes and blonde hair in twin ponytails, opened the door. The smell of freshly baked cookies made my mouth water.

Just behind the little girl was her adult version. The woman wore jeans and an extra large T-shirt. Her face was flushed and there was a dusting of flour on her nose. She was wiping her hands on a towel.

"Hi," the little girl said. "I'm Jennifer. May I help you?"

"I'm Cinnamon Greene, one of Cat Callahan's wedding photographers. I'm looking for Pastor Arneson."

"That's my dad. This is my mother," the little blond said solemnly, indicating the woman behind her. "Cat is very beautiful. When I grow up I'm going to be just like her."

I glanced at her mother, who looked horrified.

"Let's hope not," I said.

"What?" the little girl asked.

"Never mind, sweetie," her mother said quickly. "Why don't you go have a cookie?"

The little girl smiled and her small face lit up. "Okay," she said, and skipped off down the hall.

"Hi Cinnamon," the mother said. "I'm Linda. My husband is in his office at the church right now. Would you mind taking some cookies to him? I'll include a couple for you, too." She dabbed at her forehead with the towel.

"I'd do almost anything for home baked cookies. They smell wonderful."

"Come on in while I get a plate ready." As Linda turned to follow Jennifer down the hall, I noticed she was alarmingly pregnant.

"When are you due?"

"Not for another two weeks. I just hope I make it through the wedding. There's so much to do."

"I thought a women's group took care of all the things pertaining to weddings and receptions."

"It usually does," Linda replied, "but the chairperson is Megan Mauvais' mother. She and a couple of her friends feel it would be disloyal to Megan if they worked this wedding so the group is short handed."

Because of her size and condition, Linda moved down the hall awkwardly. I followed. The kitchen counters were covered with pans and mixing bowls.

Jennifer was seated at a round table, nibbling on a cookie. "May I please have some milk?" she asked.

"Of course, sweetie, but let me fix daddy's snack first. Cinnamon is going to take it to him."

"I can pour her some milk," I offered. "Where are the glasses, Jennifer?"

The little girl directed me to a cupboard and told me which glass I should take out, finishing with, "The milk is in the refrigerator door on the second shelf."

While I was carrying out my volunteer duties she said, "I'm getting a baby brother. Maybe two baby brothers. Mom's going to the hospital to get them pretty soon."

"Maybe sooner than we think," Linda said. To me she said, "My doctor insists there's only one baby but it sure feels like two. Just look at me." She turned sideways to display her awesome profile and patted her enormous belly.

Linda got out a stoneware plate, placed several cookies on it and covered it with plastic wrap.

"I usually take Don his snack," she said. "But I've got to clean up this mess and run some errands before dinner."

She handed me the plate and I said goodbye to Jennifer before we walked down the hall to the front door.

"I'll call Don and tell him you're on your way," Linda told me. "Do you know where to go?" She opened the front door.

"I think I can find it. Thanks for the cookies, Linda," I said. "See you at the wedding."

I set off toward the church. When I got near, a man came out a side door and waved at me. "Over here, Cinnamon."

Pastor Arneson didn't look like a man of the cloth. He had blond hair and blue eyes like his wife and daughter and I guessed he was only two or three years older than me. He was tall and very good looking, with a square chin and short, straight nose. He wore jeans and a sweatshirt.

He held the door open until I had gone through. "Have you been here before?" he asked as we walked down a long, dim corridor.

"Many times. Dad and I used to be regulars when I was growing up."

We reached the pastor's office. The room was good sized. It contained a large desk made of dark, highly polished wood, upon which a laptop computer sat open. Bookcases ran halfway up all but one of the four beige walls. Slightly darker carpeting covered the floor. There was a fireplace on the outside wall and sunlight poured in through the leaded glass windows on either side of it. The room was quiet and peaceful.

I handed the plate to Arneson, who removed the plastic wrap, then held it out to me. I took a cookie and sat down in one of the two brown leather chairs in front of the desk.

Arneson settled himself in the chair behind the desk. He had left the door open and now a man in orange coveralls appeared in it. He said, "Sorry, Pastor, I didn't know you had company."

"This is Cinnamon Greene, she'll be photographing Cat's wedding."

To me he said, "Chuck works for Castro Exterminators. He's been checking the grounds for bees. Cat's terribly allergic to them."

Chuck said, "Bees aren't very active this time of year. I didn't see any just now but I'll check again just before the wedding."

"Thanks, Chuck," the Pastor said. The man turned and left.

I said, "I'm surprised Cat hasn't had venom immunology. Those shots build immunity and block reaction to bee stings."

"She has," the Pastor told me. "But her parents aren't taking any chances."

"Isn't Cat allergic to some other things, too?" I asked. "I seem to remember hearing she ended up in the emergency room when she was homecoming queen."

"It was peanuts in the brownies that time," Pastor said. "Now she carries a special kit with her at all times. She injects herself with epinephrine to counteract the allergy if she feels an attack coming on."

Then he added. "What do you need from me?"

"I'd appreciate it if you could show me where things will actually take place. I haven't done this for several years and I need to check the lighting and settings. I'll need to see the Bride's Room, too."

"Let's take a walk. Want another cookie? We can eat as we go." Pastor Arneson took a cookie and held the plate out to me. I, too, took another. We left his office and walked down one hall, then another. Just off the sanctuary, he opened a door marked "Bride's Room." It had been totally redone since I was in it last and was quite suitable for a bride and her attendants, bright and cheerful. Windows high on the two outside walls above the long dressing table provided plenty of light but there were also lights around the individual mirrors that lined the table.

"The lights are a flattering pink in here so every bride is beautiful," he said, smiling.

I took my video camera out of my backpack, turned it on and panned the room. Pastor Arneson stood in the doorway and when I panned to him he smiled and waved.

When I finished I took the camera from my eye. "What's next?"

Pastor Arneson turned off the lights and we went back into the hall. Double doors leading to the sanctuary were just ahead on the left. Doors to the outside were on the right.

"I don't permit flash photos during the ceremony," Arneson told me. "Video is fine as long as you're inconspicuous. We'll reserve the end seat in the front pew on the left for you. We can do setups of the ceremony afterward for the flash photos your dad will be taking and any other video on your list."

I panned the room with my camera. When I finished I said, "Can we take a look at the reception hall?"

It was in a separate building, connected to the sanctuary by a covered walkway. It hadn't changed much since I'd seen it last. It consisted of a huge rectangular room with an equally huge kitchen on one end. On the other end there were double doors opening to the outside and restrooms. Folding doors could divide the room into several different sized spaces. On Cat's wedding day, I knew it would be transformed into a place suitable for the reception of the daughter of one the town's most prominent citizens. I panned the room with my camera before turning it off and storing it in my backpack.

"I think that's all I need, Pastor," I said. "Thanks for showing me around. And please tell Linda thanks for the delicious peanut butter cookies. They were wonderful."

"She'll be pleased to hear that," Pastor Arneson beamed. "Nice to meet you Cinnamon. You'll be at the rehearsal, won't you? See you then."

As I drove away I took one final look at the church. I had just one thought: It seemed a shame to spend all that time and money on a marriage that had no chance of succeeding.

Chapter 11

My first week in Cliffview was devoted to getting acquainted with the new store and my job at Greene's. I had grown up in Dad's store and worked part-time from junior high until I finished college. But that was years ago. Most everything had changed. Luckily, because I had worked for a photographer, I was up to date technically and knew what products were available for pro photographers. There was still a lot to learn, however, and new staff members to get to know.

I worked every day my first week. Dad had plans for the second week.

"You need some time off, honey. Why don't you come diving with me on Wednesday?"

While I had been an avid scuba diver in high school and college I had gone only occasionally since then, usually on the Friday after Thanksgiving. Ted and I spent that holiday weekend in Cliffview. While Dad and I were diving he visited college buddies.

"My wetsuit is old and stiff," I reminded Dad. "I need a new one and my regulator needs an overhaul."

Dad said, "You can rent a wetsuit and any other equipment you need and have your regulator tuned at the dive store. It's under new management."

During my lunch hour I visited Cliffview Divers and rented a few pieces of equipment from its owner, Danny Decker. He said he'd bring the tuned-up regulator and the rental equipment to the boat because he was going on the Wednesday trip, too.

My first impressions of Danny weren't all that favorable. While he was undeniably attractive, I've never been fond of goatees and was confused by the small gold ring in his left ear. Did it mean he was gay?

Dad said he'd pick me up at 6:00 am the day of trip. I didn't know Sandy was going until I got in his truck. She greeted me with a smile.

Neither Dad nor I are morning people. We're not at all sociable until we've had something to eat and at least one cup of coffee. Sandy must be the same way. We sipped coffee and ate the scones Dad had picked up at The Bakery as we drove the ten minutes north to Santa Barbara. There was no conversation.

At the harbor, Dad parked in the big lot near the landing and we busied ourselves carting gear to the *California Diver*.

The first person we saw on the boat was Paul Patterson.

"Hey Red," he called. "You really are getting old. How much you paying those Sherpas to lug your gear?"

"Your green eyes are showing, you old coot," Dad fired back. "I've got two lovely young buddies and you're stuck with ol' Pete."

Pete Johnson, a retired Cliffview High P.E. teacher in his 60s, appeared in the galley door. "Hey," he said, sounding hurt.

"Sorry, Pete," Dad said. "But you aren't young and beautiful anymore."

"Beauty is as beauty does," Pete replied. "At the end of the day it's who's got the most lobster that counts."

"Put your money where your mouth is," someone demanded and suddenly everyone stopped what they were doing to fish wallets out of their pockets and come up with dollar bills. Paul produced a small notepad and a ballpoint pen and began recording the names of the bettors while Pete collected the money. I remembered that for the "Mostest" pool, divers picked the person they thought would catch the most lobsters. Most bet on themselves. Sandy and I bet on Dad.

When the gear was stowed I took a quick tour of the *California Diver*. A state of the art fiberglass boat, she was designed and built for diving. Although her blue and white paint was new, her other features, a below decks shower room and the three heads on the main deck, were familiar. I headed for the below decks bunkroom. I was wrapped in a blanket before the boat left the dock and cruised out of the harbor toward Santa Cruz Island. The cool, early morning air and the drone of diesel engines made me drowsy. I fell asleep immediately.

The sound of the anchor going overboard woke me. Rubbing sleep from my eyes, I rolled out of the bunk and went topside.

The sun shone bright in a clear blue sky and the ocean was unusually calm. The boat deck was a beehive of activity, with divers pulling on wetsuits and drysuits, assembling buoyancy compensators and regulators on tanks, checking computers and purging second stages. I felt a tingle of anticipation and apprehension. I found my gear bag and began getting ready.

Sandy, Dad and I were nearly dressed when Danny Decker walked up, carrying my regulator. "Good as new," he said, adding, "Do you have a buddy? If not, you can dive with me."

Sandy said, "That's a great idea, Cinnamon."

"Or, you can dive with us," Dad said.

"Threesomes are a bad idea," Sandy reminded us.

Before I could reply Dad said, "You're right. I'll be your buddy, Cinnamon. Sandy can dive with Danny."

Sandy and Danny exchanged not-so-happy looks.

"Dad," I said, "Danny's an instructor. I'll be fine."

"Don't worry, Red, I'll take good care of her," Danny said.

Dad looked uncomfortable but the decision had been made. When I'd been in his shop, Danny had been busy and I'd been preoccupied. Now, as he walked off to finish gearing up, I stole a glance at him. Thick wetsuits accentuate figure flaws; Danny's trim, muscular body had none that I could see.

Suddenly Danny turned and looked at me. He grinned wickedly and winked. I decided he wasn't gay. I blushed and quickly focused on connecting my regulator to my tank. I put it on upside down the first time.

When he returned, Danny and I did a buddy check to familiarize ourselves with each other's gear and discussed our dive plan.

As we lined up at the bow, ready to jump in the water, Dad made one more try, "Why don't the four of us dive together?" Behind facemasks, three pairs of eyes looked at him and three mouths said "No" simultaneously.

Sandy jumped in first, followed by Dad, Danny and me. I had forgotten how cold 59°F water was but very quickly remembered as it seeped into my wetsuit. The visibility was about 50 feet, which was excellent for the Northern Channel Islands. Dad and Sandy were below us, headed for the bottom at 60 feet. While Dad's gear was all black Sandy's was distinctive; she had a pink mask and snorkel, a pink tank and a pink and black wetsuit. When she and Dad reached the sand, they finned off toward the kelp forest on our right.

On the bottom, Danny led the way with me following.

When the initial awkwardness wore off, I felt as if I had never been away from diving. I was quickly reminded why I loved it. The only sounds we heard were the exhaled air from our regulators and the constant crackling of the tiny snapping shrimp that live on the bottom of the ocean. The noise they make stuns their prey so they can eat it.

Sunbeams danced down through gently swaying kelp fronds; fish flitted hither and yon and it was, in a word, beautiful. I was so busy looking around that I forgot I had a buddy. When I looked for him, he was gone.

Danny is an instructor and I knew he'd be back. To make myself easier to find, I ascended a few feet and grabbed onto a kelp stipe. I had barely done so when I saw him headed toward me, looking side to side frantically. I let go of the stipe and drifted down in front of him. When we set off once more we paid more attention to each other. That was important to me because the only diving skill I have never managed to master is navigation. (I don't navigate well on land, either.) It's a genetic defect, handed down from mother to daughter, according to Dad.

Danny and I wandered here and there among the kelp, searching rocky cracks and crevices for lobsters. I noticed that Danny's game bag already held one. While West Coast bugs don't have claws like their Eastern cousins, they're not defenseless. They have sharp spines on their bodies and the ability to scoot backward through the water with amazing speed. I found two and pointed them out to Danny who bagged them. When my confidence returned, I'd try grabbing them myself.

About 25 minutes into the dive I began to feel cold. A minute or so later, Danny pointed out the anchor line. We ascended to 15 feet, making a three-minute safety stop before surfacing and swimming to the platform at the stern of the boat.

On the dive platform, Danny held up our bag. "You raised a hell of a lobster finder, Red," he said, "And, as you can see, I brought her back in one piece. How did you do?"

"We got skunked," Dad admitted. "But that was only the first dive. We'll catch up."

Danny and I made two more dives that day. In between we ordered lunch from the crew members staffing the galley, drank cups of herbal tea, hot cider and hot chocolate to warm us up and swapped stories (Danny seemed to have a lot of them) with the other divers. I felt very comfortable with him, both in and out of the water.

Although I found a lobster on our last dive, I

hesitated a fraction of a second before grabbing it and it jetted backward through the kelp. I finned after it and attempted two more grabs but all I got was part of an antenna. Danny and I laughed so much our masks filled up with water.

"Just you wait," I told him on the deck afterward, "I'm a little rusty now. I'll get the next one."

"Sure you will," Danny teased, that wicked grin in place. "And I bet you think the Cubs are going to win the World Series."

Dad and Danny buddied up for the fourth dive, while Sandy and I got out of our wetsuits. We were too cold to go into the water again. Taking a hot shower and putting on dry, warm clothes felt wonderful. Afterward, as I sat sipping coffee in the galley, Sandy came in and fixed herself a cup of hot chocolate. She smiled at me before wandering outside.

The next thing I knew, Dad and Danny were standing in the galley doorway, both of them grinning idiotically. Divers crowded around them.

"Look what we got," Dad said. He could hardly contain himself as he held up a good-sized lobster.

"Omigod, Red, it's huge," Sandy exclaimed.

"Must be a least ten pounds," I said. "Who caught it?"

The men looked at each other, still grinning. "You tell 'em, Red," Danny said.

"No, you tell 'em, Danny."

"I insist, you first."

"I'll tell 'em," Paul Patterson said. He stepped out from behind Dad and Danny and took the bug. "After all, it's my bug. And I got my limit so I win

—

67

the Mostest pool, too."

Dad and Danny took off their wetsuits and put their gear away. After they showered and dressed in dry clothes, they joined Sandy, me, Paul and Pete at a table in the galley. When we neared the harbor, everyone scattered to get their gear together. Once I had mine collected in one spot, I went to the bow. I loved watching all the activities as we motored to the dock. Danny joined me there.

"We should do this again soon," he said. "The only way to improve your lobster grabbing skills is to go diving more often with a buddy who has mastered the art and can show you how it's done." His tone was mock-serious.

Those dark blue eyes were disconcerting. "Dad's already got a buddy," I teased adding, "I had forgotten how much I enjoy lobster diving."

Sandy and Dad walked up. "Sandy and I are having a lobster feast tomorrow night," he told us. "You're both invited."

"Hey, that'd be great," Danny said. "I'll bring two of ours so there'll be enough. That way I'll only owe Cinnamon half of one." He looked at me. "Let me know when you want me to cook it for you. Or," he winked, "you can cook it for me."

"Believe me," I said. "It won't be edible if I cook it."

"Cinnamon specializes in microwaving chicken noodle soup and frozen dinners," Dad said.

"Hey," I countered. "I can also toast a pretty mean peanut butter sandwich."

The boat docked and we lugged gear back to Dad's truck. Before Danny drove off in his van, we set a time for dinner the next night.

On the way home I asked, "What's the deal with Danny? Is he married? Gay?"

Dad laughed. "He's divorced, has a son, and he's definitely not gay. The pirate look is fairly new. Paul calls him 'Captain Kidd,' which everybody but Danny thinks is hilarious. He can't get rid of the goatee and the earring now until he thinks we've forgotten about them."

Dad and Sandy were going to his place, where they planned to order pizza. I was invited, too, but I suddenly realized I was dead tired. There's nothing like a day on and in the ocean to wear one out. Dad dropped me off at my condo, where I took a nice long hot shower, then filled the bathtub with water and dumped my gear in it to soak. Afterward I hung everything out on the balcony to dry.

For dinner, I had my specialty; canned chicken noodle soup and a toasted peanut butter sandwich.

Not much later I slipped into my sleeping bag with the newest Sue Grafton paperback. While I tried to concentrate on the incredible antics of the heroine, Kinsey Millhone, my eyes just wouldn't stay open.

Chapter 12

Jilted Lover read the directions on the back of the cake mix box one more time. The pans were greased and floured and the oven was already heated to 350°F. The ingredients were assembled: cake mix, water, oil, eggs and one-quarter cup of a finely ground substance. One of The Bakery's pink boxes, only slightly used, sat empty and waiting nearby.

Jilted Lover knew the cake only needed to look like the layer it would replace. That should be easy enough to do because the Cliffview Chronicle had printed an interview with Veronica in which she had described the number and size of the layers and when and where the cake would be baked as well as who would decorate it and when. Those details were very helpful.

Jilted Lover opened the box containing the chocolate cake mix and ripped open the plastic bag, dumping the brown powder into the mixing bowl. Water, oil, eggs and the finely ground substance were added. Jilted Lover turned on the mixer and watched the batter become a dark, shiny brown before pouring the batter into the pans and placing them in the oven.

In a few minutes a delicious aroma filled the room. Jilted Lover sniffed the air and smiled. One special person would find this cake deadly.

Chapter 13

After work the next day, I showered and changed into khakis and a T-shirt before heading to Sandy's. I arrived just after Dad. Danny showed up a few minutes later, with two lobster tails and a bottle of white wine. He wore clean jeans and a short-sleeved shirt with a muted tropical flower pattern. His hair was still damp from his shower and he smelled of aftershave. He greeted me with a smile.

Sandy had prepared a platter of raw veggies with dip. She and Dad sat on the couch, Danny and I sat cross legged on the floor. We nibbled veggies and drank wine while the two men regaled us with tales of previous lobster dives, parts of which may even have been true. Then Sandy gave the guys a platter of lobster tails and sent them out to the deck to cook them on the barbecue. She and I made a salad, melted butter to dip the lobster meat in, steamed some fresh green beans and heated some wheat rolls.

Before long, Dad stuck his head in the door. "Five minutes more. Are you ready?"

Dinner was delicious. It had been a long time since I'd had lobster that was not only fresh but perfectly cooked. I savored every mouthful. The conversation revolved around various ways to cook lobster and other seafood as well as the demise of once-plenty abalone.

Then I had a thought. "Do you still take underwater photos, Dad?"

"Of course. Just not during lobster season."

Danny looked at me. "Are you an underwater photographer?"

"I used to be."

"She won several contests when she was in high school. Her art teacher said her work was professional quality," Dad said proudly.

Danny looked impressed.

"Be careful, Dad," I warned. "I'll get a big head and insist you pay me more money."

"I could never pay you what you're worth, honey."

Several minutes later, I looked at the clock on the kitchen wall. "I'm going to head on home, guys. Thanks for dinner, Sandy."

Dad stood up. "I'll walk you home."

Sandy looked surprised.

Danny said, "It's time I was leaving, too. I can give you a lift, Cinnamon."

"Great," I said. Sandy looked relieved.

I didn't have to tell Danny where I lived, he already knew.

"Nothing's a secret in Cliffview," he said. "Everyone knows you rented the last empty condo in the North Beach compound."

"I'm not sure I like living in a small town again. My soon to be ex-husband is a celebrity but I was pretty anonymous in LA."

Danny pulled up to the curb in front of my condo.

"Tonight was fun," he said. "Want to go to a movie tomorrow night?"

"I can't. Cat's rehearsal is tomorrow night and

there's a dinner afterward." I tried not to sound as disappointed as I felt.

"And the wedding's Saturday so that's out," Danny finished. "How about Sunday night?"

"Deal," I said.

"I'll call you Sunday afternoon and we can decided what we want to see then," he said.

I was about to say "Great" but Danny's lips got in the way. While the kiss surprised me, its intensity scared me. An electric shock traveled through my body like a bolt of lightning. When we finally parted, my heart was beating so fast and loud I was sure Danny could hear it.

I gulped a great breath of air. "So that's settled," I said giddily. "See you Sunday." Self-preservation propelled me out of the truck and up the walk to my condo. My last glimpse of Danny's face, pale in the glow of the streetlight, showed what I took to be astonishment. I turned just before I went into the lobby and waved. Danny sat motionless in his truck.

Ignoring the elevator, I floated up the steps to my condo. Once inside, I got ready for bed, trying not to think too much about what had just happened. It was way too soon to attach much importance to one kiss, even one that left me breathless.

Chapter 14

I awoke the next day knowing Danny had figured prominently in my dreams but unable to remember them. I whistled "High Hopes" while I fixed breakfast. That had never happened before. As I ate, I wondered if my subconscious was trying to tell me something via the song.

It was Friday and everyone seemed to be preparing for a photographic weekend. The store was busy. Just after 6:00 pm, Dad and I collected the equipment we needed for the wedding rehearsal and left the store. He dropped me at my condo, where I changed into a pair of navy slacks and a pale blue silk blouse. He picked me up an hour later and we drove to the church.

We were the first ones there by a matter of minutes. At the appointed time, everyone who was supposed to be there was. Pastor Arneson explained the sequence of events. His daughter, Jennifer, sat next to me in the pew with Mrs. Arneson, who looked as if she would deliver any minute. Jennifer's big blue eyes followed Cat adoringly, as did the eyes of her fiancé, Chip. Cat, as always, looked spectacular. Wearing a green silk blouse and black slacks, she was movie star beautiful and knew it.

The rehearsal proceeded chaotically. Giggling and confusion abounded. Things improved a bit after Pastor Arneson gently but firmly wrested control of the proceedings from Margo Callahan. Perhaps sensing his role was merely supportive, Mayor Callahan kept an uncharacteristically low profile.

I filmed a few key moments to use at the beginning of the wedding video.

At one point I whispered to Dad, sitting next to me in a pew, "The wedding will be a disaster. These people can't do anything right."

"You've forgotten," he said. "Rehearsals are always like this. Yet somehow the weddings come off near perfect."

It was a relief when the bride and groom said make believe "I dos" and the run-through was over. We said good-bye to the Arnesons, piled into our vehicles and headed for Jonathan's.

The dinner was even more chaotic. Everyone was in high spirits and the wine served with dinner only intensified them. It was a boisterous wedding party and, in the morning, some of its members would regret imbibing so much. Dad and I quickly ate our dinners and escaped before dessert. I had a splitting headache.

Before I went to bed I checked my voice messages, finding one from Danny. It was short and to the point: "Sunday can't come too soon. See you then, Cinnamon."

The headache was gone when I fell asleep and there was a smile on my face.

Chapter 15

Day had not yet dawned when Jilted Lover parked the luxury vehicle in front of a condominium complex. After locking the car, Jilted Lover placed its remote control in a pants pocket. Dressed in black watch cap, black sweatpants and black sweatshirt, Jilted Lover crossed the street and began power walking south. The streetlights were barely visible through the thick fog. While it dampened sound, Jilted Lover's thick soled running shoes wouldn't have made noise anyway.

At the end of the block, Jilted Lover turned toward the ocean. After another block, a large expanse of carefully manicured lawn came into view. Jilted Lover walked toward the westernmost building, the one closest to the cliff. There, Jilted Lover tried the front door and found it locked. Jilted Lover walked quickly along the ocean side of the building toward the back. Although the back door was also locked, one of the windows was slightly ajar and easily opened. Jilted Lover put a small cake box through the window and set it on a table. Then Jilted Lover climbed through the window and closed it.

A few minutes later, Jilted Lover reappeared in the doorway carrying the small box, making sure no one was around before leaving the building. Jilted Lover jogged back to the car but on arriving there could not find its keyless remote. When none of the pockets in the sweatsuit yielded the key, Jilted Lover *started to retrace the original route. Within a block, however, the fog began to lift. As the sun rose in the sky, the streetlights blinked off.*

Even though it was still early, the risk of being seen was too great. That would be disastrous. The black clad Jilted Lover turned and jogged back toward the car, passed it and kept on going.

Chapter 16

The day of the wedding dawned bright and clear. I got to the church earlier than I planned. Carrying my video camera, I checked out the sanctuary and the Bride's Room (which showed no sign of the bride or her attendants), then wandered over to the reception hall. That was a beehive of activity. I found Linda Arneson in the kitchen. Due to deliver at any second, she looked tired and frazzled.

"Should you be here?" I asked.

"No," one of the women said. While I recognized her as a long time Cliffview resident I couldn't remember her name. "We keep telling her we don't have time to deliver a baby," the woman continued. She said it jokingly, but there was concern in her voice. "Why don't you let Cinnamon escort you home, Linda?"

I opened the back door of the building with a flourish and made a little bow. "After you madame," I said, looking at Linda.

She hesitated just a fraction of a second before walking through the doorway. "See you later," she said to the women. "Thanks a bunch."

"Go home and put your feet up," one of the women said. "We can handle this."

When we were outside I said, "You look as if you're going to have that baby any minute."

"I'm sure it won't be much longer," she admitted.

An idea struck me. "Why don't I take a short 'before' video? I can take an 'after' video when you're nice and slim again."

"That may never happen. I've gained 50 pounds. Ten more than I gained with Jennifer."

"Stand over there," I directed, pointing toward a spot on the grass. I turned on my camera and aimed it at Linda. "Face the camera and then turn slowly to your left so I can get a profile."

Linda did as I asked. "How do I look? Quite svelte?"

"I'd say you look pretty good for a woman who swallowed the Goodyear Blimp. Maybe there is more than one in there."

"Bite your tongue," Linda commanded. "Want to see me walk?" She turned her back to me and did a comically exaggerated waddle.

"I'm impressed you're still so mobile," I said, laughing. "Now what are you doing? I'm not sure you should be dancing."

Linda was doing a funny little two-step with her eyes trained on the ground. "I just stepped on something hard," she said. "My belly's so big I can't see what it is and I couldn't bend over to pick it up even if I could see it. Help me out here."

I zoomed down and focused on the object at her feet before walking over and picking it up. Partially embedded in the ground was a car's keyless remote.

"Here's your mystery object," I said, noting the remote's distinctive logo. "Know anyone who owns a BMW?"

"It must belong to someone working in the hall. I'll go ask."

"Oh no you won't," I said. "You're going home. I'll see if I can find the owner of the remote."

"Okay," she said, sounding relieved. "You don't have to go with me, it's just a short distance. I'll see you later." She turned and walked off.

In the kitchen I asked if anyone had lost a BMW keyless remote. No one claimed it. I asked again in the hall with the same result. After a glance at my watch I hightailed it over to the Bride's Room. A couple of the bridesmaids arrived a few minutes later. Two more straggled in during the next 15 minutes. The bride, her mother and the maid of honor finally showed up about 45 minutes later.

What happened in the next hour exceeded my worst expectations. The din created by the women escalated in inverse proportion to the time left before the ceremony. A maelstrom whirled around Cat. Three times she sent her mother back to her condo to retrieve some essential she'd left behind. While Margo was not thrilled about the last two times, she remained calm, although I could see it took a lot of effort.

It wasn't all Cat, however. The maid of honor worried out loud about a zit on her nose. Another of the bridesmaids turned out to be allergic to the flowers in the room and kept sneezing. A call to Mrs. Arneson saved the day. She had Jennifer deliver an antihistamine to alleviate the symptoms. As the little girl was leaving, I remembered the BMW remote.

"Anyone here have a BMW? I yelled above the din. I had to ask three times before I got an answer.

All present yelled "No," simultaneously.

"Jennifer," I said, "please give this remote to

your mother. Tell her I couldn't find the owner."

"Okay," the little girl answered, her eyes on the bride. If I hadn't shooed her out the door, she would have stayed and admired Cat forever.

It was then that the room reached meltdown.

I was videoing the final stage of Cat's transition from pretty woman in curlers and jeans to beautiful bride when she began rummaging around in the pile of litter at her feet. "Where are my pantyhose?" she demanded, her face creased in a frown.

In various stages of undress, no one paid any attention. Even Margo was oblivious, touching up her make-up in the mirror.

"Where are my pantyhose?" Cat said louder.

There was still no reply.

"Where are my pantyhose?" Cat screamed. "If I can't find my pantyhose I can't get married."

Everyone froze and there was a dead silence before all of the women rushed to surround Cat. "Take mine," three voices entreated and three bridesmaids held out pairs of pink pantyhose. The maid of honor and the fourth bridesmaid, already wearing theirs, looked stricken.

"I can't wear pink, you idiots," Cat shrieked. "They have to be black."

"They must be here somewhere. Everybody look," Margo commanded. I could hear panic in her voice.

Six women began shuffling through the mountains of clothes and boxes that covered every available surface. I continued shooting, fascinated.

After a few minutes of frantic activity, the maid of honor held up a package of black panty hose. "I found them," she announced triumphantly.

Everyone looked at Cat.

"I knew they were here somewhere. Guess I'll be getting married after all." Cat allowed a small smile to grace her face.

That's when I realized why Margo had held her temper in check and everyone had rushed to Cat's side. They were all afraid there would be a repeat of her last wedding, when she left her groom standing at the altar. Cat knew her trump card and was taking full advantage of it.

Yet somehow, some way, the bride and her attendants were dressed and ready only a few minutes after the ceremony was supposed to begin.

When everyone had left the Bride's Room, I did a slow pan of it with my video camera. There were female garments, plastic bags, shoe and flower boxes strewn everywhere. The place looked as if it had been struck by a tornado, which in fact it had. A tornado named Cat.

Chapter 17

As the bridal attendants lined up outside the sanctuary with the ring bearer and flower girls, the mayor of Cliffview arrived. Under his adoring gaze, his daughter blossomed into a radiant, albeit nontraditional, bride.

At the first note of the wedding march, the guests turned and looked at Cat, then let out an audible sigh. It wasn't just the bridal party that was relieved to see this wedding would take place.

As far as I could tell, everything went perfectly, although the groom nearly fainted when he looked at his intended. She was, indeed, absolutely stunning in her wedding gown.

After the ceremony, the guests walked across the grounds to the reception hall while the wedding party re-enacted parts of the ceremony for photos shot by Dad and video shot by me. About 45 minutes later, we all joined the reception. The champagne had already been flowing and the guests, about 300 in all, were in great spirits.

Cliffview's best restaurant, Jonathan's, which had also hosted the rehearsal dinner, had produced a lavish buffet and as soon as the wedding party arrived the guests pounced upon it.

Dad and I did not have time to eat. Margo had supplied a list of friends and relatives of the bride and groom (mostly the bride, it seemed). I interviewed these people on camera, recording their well wishes.

Dad took candid shots.

We photographed numerous toasts to the couple and got ready to photograph the pair feeding each other wedding cake. Veronica and Georgia had outdone themselves. The cake was five spectacular layers high. Decorated with pink roses and topped by a miniature bride and groom, it was magnificent.

Chip went first, taking a small slice from the topmost "Anniversary Layer" and holding it up so Cat could nibble on it. Dad and I had great spots for video and stills.

"Have some more, Cat," Margo Callahan urged. "We want to make sure we get good photos."

Cat obliged as Dad's strobe flashed and my video camera recorded the deed. After Cat fed Chip his slice the band started playing. While everyone watched, the mayor led his daughter out on the floor for their special dance. I filmed them as they moved expertly around the hall. When Chip cut in, the mayor graciously surrendered his daughter to her new husband. Many guests joined the couple on the dance floor while others began queuing up for a piece of the cake, which had been sliced into pieces in the kitchen.

Not long after the newlyweds started dancing, however, Cat began scratching one of her arms. Through my lens I noticed her face was flushed and her eyes were wide open. She seemed to be trying to tell Chip something only no words came out. She put both hands on her throat, opened her mouth and began gasping for air. As I watched, she collapsed in a black silk heap. Chip caught her and managed to slow her descent to the floor, where she lay still.

Stunned, I continued filming.

Margo pushed through the crowd, flung herself down on the floor next to her daughter and screamed, "She's having an allergic reaction. Where's her allergy kit? Cassidy," she directed the maid of honor, "go look in the Bride's Room. Hurry. Someone call 911. Is there a doctor in the house?"

Margo's panicky instructions mobilized the guests. The maid of honor flew off to the Bride's Room; cell phones sprouted in every hand; and every doctor in the room (there were at least six) headed toward the bride. None of the doctors, however, had a medical bag. Orders were issued; kids and wives sprinted from the room.

My camera remained an extension of my eyes. Chip and Margo knelt helplessly beside Cat, each holding one of her hands, their faces white with shock. Suddenly, I was shoved out of the way. Mayor Callahan and several of his close friends formed a ring around the prostrate bride while other men herded the guests outside. There, little groups formed, whispering among themselves or talking on cell phones. Somehow, Dad and I managed to locate each other.

"They'll never find the allergy kit in the Bride's Room," I told him, keeping my voice low. "It's in total chaos."

Dad looked as shocked as I felt. "I hope someone can help," he said. "I can't imagine what happened. Veronica baked the cake and she knows about her niece's allergies, everyone in town does."

Within minutes after we were hustled outside, sirens and blazing lights heralded the arrival of emergency crews. As the trucks came to a stop in the parking lot, personnel jumped out and ran inside the building. Several minutes later, we heard Margo Callahan's agonized scream and knew that her daughter had died.

The door of the hall opened and a haggard Pastor Arneson appeared. There was sudden silence and the guests looked at him expectantly. "Go home, everybody," he said. "There's nothing anyone can do now."

Dad called Sandy and told her what had happened as I drove back to Greene's. I called Danny when we got there but he didn't answer his cell. I didn't leave a message, figuring I'd call him a little later. However, when Dad and I began unloading our equipment from the van and putting it away our phones started ringing constantly. It seemed everyone who hadn't gone to the wedding was calling us. In order to get photos and video downloaded to our computers and backed up, we turned off our phones.

When we finished, Dad drove me to my condo. Both of us were exhausted. As I walked up the stairs to the lobby, I remembered how I had felt less than 24 hours before. Then I was flying. Now I was crashing. What a difference a day makes.

Chapter 18

I had trouble sleeping that night and when I did, images of the bride, hands clutching her throat, kept appearing in my dreams. Just after I finally fell into a deep sleep, however, the alarm clock went off. Without opening my eyes I reached out and hit the snooze button. The buzzing persisted.

I finally realized the noise was the doorbell. I stumbled to the door and threw it open, intending to give whoever was disturbing me this early an earful. While that was my plan, it dissolved when I saw Danny standing there. He looked concerned, anxious and uncomfortable.

"What?" I grumbled.

Danny held up a bag. "I brought chocolate croissants and coffee," he said hopefully. "I left several messages on your phone."

I stood there blinking at him.

"Can I come in? You'll cold catch cold standing out here dressed like that." He grinned and I realized that all I wore was a short white T-shirt and a pair of bikini panties.

I moved aside so Danny could come in. He closed the door as I hustled off to the bedroom. I slipped into a pair of jeans and a sweatshirt, splashed my face with cold water and combed my hair before returning to the living room. Danny had made himself at home at my breakfast bar, munching on a croissant and sipping coffee.

"Feeling better?" he asked.

I nodded. "Coffee now, talk later."

We sat in silence for a while. Finally I said: "I didn't sleep very well last night."

"I'm not surprised," Danny said. "Quite a few people who'd been at the wedding showed up at Flanagan's last night and I heard all about it. I called and when you didn't answer, I drove by here. Your windows were dark."

"It's so bizarre, Danny. Everyone knows about Cat's allergies. How could something like this happen?"

"Some think it was done on purpose."

"Murder?" I was incredulous.

"Cat loves to go after guys who belong to other people," Danny said. "She broke up more than one marriage, including Sandy's."

"Chip dumped Megan for her," I remembered.

"And she dumped Sandy's ex, Jason, for Chip," Danny reminded me. "But they're just a few of the many victims."

"You, too?" I asked with sudden insight.

He glanced sharply at me and hesitated before answering.

"Yes," he admitted reluctantly. "I had just bought Cliffview Divers. I was commuting from Ventura. Things were not great between my wife and me. She was upset that I'd used the money I inherited to buy a dive store. She wanted a house.

"When my scuba students pass their certification course we celebrate at Flanagan's. That's where Cat started flirting with me. She was ten years younger and so beautiful. It was extremely flattering. We spent a couple of nights together. My wife found out and filed for divorce. Cat moved on to her next victim.

"I watched her manipulate Jason and Chip. Believe me, it was quite an education."

"Were you in love with her?" I asked, feeling a sharp pang of jealousy.

Danny gave a short laugh. "Love had nothing to do with it. It was a game to Cat. She enjoyed making conquests. When I look back on it I don't know how I could have been so stupid. Those two nights were not worth the loss of my family."

"Someday I'll tell you how it feels to be made a fool of on national TV," I said.

Before he could ask about that, I changed the subject. "How old is your son?"

Danny's face lit up. "Sam is seven. He lives with his mom in Ventura and spends one night a week and every other weekend with me."

I looked at Danny's watch. "It's late. I've got to get going. Shouldn't you be at your store?"

"My part-time instructor opened it this morning. But I should show up pretty soon. Can I drop you at the mall?"

As we were leaving a few minutes later, Danny gently enfolded me in his arms. "I've been wanting to do this all morning."

I put my arms around his waist. "Why did you wait so long?"

"I was afraid you'd slug me," he said. "You're quite something first thing in the morning. I liked the outfit, the attitude I could do without."

We ended the embrace with a long kiss and walked down the steps to the street hand in hand.

—

On the way to Greene's, we agreed to meet at my condo after work. We'd go to dinner and watch a movie at his place afterward.

As I was getting out of his truck, Danny said: "I almost forgot. Linda Arneson had her baby last night. It was a boy. Eight pounds seven ounces."

"Wow, that's big. When?"

"About 9:00 pm. I heard about it at The Bakery this morning. Mother and baby are doing fine."

When I got to Greene's I started to tell Dad about the baby but he already knew. News travels fast in a small town. Just how fast I was soon to find out. We were swamped all day. Most of the people weren't customers, however, they were locals who hadn't been at the wedding and hoped to get the details from someone who had. Those who had been at the reception knew I had recorded Cat's last moments and either hinted around or asked outright if they could see what I'd shot.

Dad had known we'd get crowds of the curious. His standard, and truthful, reply was, "We turned the video over to the police. We haven't had a chance to view it." He'd taken a copy of my video to the police before he opened the store.

Our phone rang constantly. Everyone was hoping we would tell him or her something no one else knew.

By the time we closed shop that day, my throat was sore from nonstop talking. Before he dropped me at my condo, Dad told me he and Sandy were going to dinner in Santa Barbara. When they got home he was going to mute his phone and go to bed. "They call me, you know, no matter what time it is. You're lucky only a few people know your number."

———

"I think I'll keep it that way for awhile," I croaked as I got out of the car. "See you tomorrow."

A hot shower and two glasses of water revived me somewhat, though I knew I wasn't going to be the liveliest of companions that night.

When Danny rang the doorbell, I hugged him and explained what had happened that day. My throat hurt and I could barely talk.

"We don't have to go out. We can order in and watch a movie."

"I'd like that," I rasped.

"We'll have to go to my place, however," he said, "since you don't have a TV or a sofa."

"I don't even have a bed," I said and felt my face burn.

Danny looked at me and grinned his evil grin. "Really. Now that's most unfortunate."

"Don't read anything into that," I protested. "It's just a comment on my lack of furniture."

"I'm sure it is." The grin remained on his face. He did, however, change the subject. "What's your pleasure: pizza, Chinese, Japanese, Mexican?"

"You choose," I said. "What I want more than anything is a cold beer."

"We can order a pizza and have it delivered. I've got beer at home."

"Sounds good."

Danny drove me to the tiny little house he was buying on the east side of the Pacific Coast Highway. Though he warned me it was a fixer upper, it was neat and clean inside and out. When he showed me around there was pride in his voice. The house was 50 years old and had two bedrooms, one of which was Sam's, one small bathroom and a kitchen Danny was in the process of modernizing.

"I'm going to work on the bathroom next," he said. "Eventually, I'll add a master bedroom and bath."

The backyard was fenced and Danny had built a tree house in the large pepper tree. The little boy's room looked well used and comfortable.

"Sam will be here next weekend," Danny said. "You can meet him then. He's really smart. You'll like him."

"Uh, uh," I said, reserving judgment.

Danny led me into the living room, insisted I sit down on the sofa, and poured me a beer. Then he handed me the remote for the TV. He ordered a pizza before joining me on the sofa with his own beer. The cold brew tasted good and I drank it rather quickly. The pizza arrived and we devoured it at Danny's kitchen table. Later, while I tried to watch the movie we'd chosen, my eyes kept closing.

Chapter 19

I awoke to the smell of coffee. At first I didn't know where I was, which was on Danny's sofa. I peeled off the blanket that was wrapped around me and sat up.

"You're a great date," Danny said cheerfully. "Super easy to please."

I stared at him groggily.

"Don't worry; you don't have to talk before you've had your coffee." He poured me a cup and brought it over.

"Morning, Sunshine," he said, setting the cup down on the coffee table.

"Must you be so cheerful?"

"Sorry, I'll try to be more grouchy."

"Please." I didn't mean it and he knew it.

"We had one hell of a day," I said. "I don't think I can go through another one like it."

"It'll be better today. You've had your 15 minutes of fame, you're old news now. The Cliffview grapevine claims the cops are about to arrest either Veronica, her daughter Georgia or both for poisoning the wedding cake."

"Cat's aunt and cousin? That's ridiculous. They both adored her."

"Well," Danny said, "Some people think Georgia only pretended to be fond of Cat and that she was actually incredibly jealous of her."

"I don't believe that. I've known Georgia a long

time. She is one of the nicest women I've ever met. There's not a mean bone in her body."

Danny shrugged. "I agree. The cops were searching The Bakery this morning so I had to buy bagels at the grocery store. That's where I ran into Sandy. She told me a Cliffview policeman is dating a woman who works in her office. He claims they're pretty sure Cat's death was caused by a severe allergic reaction to something she ate, most probably the wedding cake. They're having the cake, the frosting and the contents of Cat's stomach analyzed. Also," Danny continued, "Veronica admits she baked the cake. Some think she could be covering for Georgia."

"I think the whole thing's ludicrous," I said. "Sweet Aunt Veronica and mild mannered Georgia, murderers?" I shuddered.

"Well anyway, now you know what you slept through. Are you diving with us Wednesday?"

"I thought there was only one Warriors trip a month."

"There are two in October and November because of lobster season."

"Let me check with my boss. But sure, I'd like to go. The trip last week was fun."

Danny toasted a bagel for me and I ate it with cream cheese. Before we left his house, he gave me a hug and a long kiss. He dropped me off at my condo, where I washed my face and reapplied my mascara. I also changed my clothes. The ones I was wearing looked as if they had been slept in.

Danny was right, business was underwhelming at Greene's. The gossips had moved on, with the phone ringing off the hook at The Bakery, which opened just before lunch. Business boomed there as locals crowded in, hoping for a chance to talk to Veronica or Georgia. Greene's employee Mike Takamura tried to buy his usual sandwich there and couldn't get in the front door because there were so many people inside.

I told Dad what Danny had predicted, then asked if he and Sandy were going on the Wednesday dive. He said they were signed up in perpetuity on Warriors dives. He was pleased to hear I wanted to go.

"I was hoping you'd get back into diving," he told me. "All of your underwater photo gear is obsolete though."

"I've got good cameras but will definitely need a new housing and strobes. Which reminds me, what are you going to do with Cat's wedding photos?"

"I'm going to fill the order the Callahans paid for and wait for them to tell me when they want it. It may be a while before they're ready."

Even though we weren't as busy as we'd been the previous day, the hours passed quickly. Mayor Callahan called Dad in late afternoon. He wanted to see the wedding video. Dad grew agitated when he told me about it

"The mayor is in a panic," he said. "Several hours ago Chief Lawson took his sister and niece to the police station and has been interviewing them because during their search of The Bakery they found a packet of ground peanuts. They think either Veronica or Georgia, maybe both, baked nuts into the wedding cake, knowing Cat was allergic to them.

"The mayor tried to get Veronica and Georgia to hire a lawyer he recommended but they told him there's no need, they are innocent. He hopes there is something in the video that proves his sister and niece didn't do what the cops think they did."

I interrupted him. "Chief Lawson must have rocks in his head to suspect Veronica and Georgia. They're incapable of harming anyone. Besides, nuts are a common ingredient in baked goods. You'd expect to find them in most bakeries."

"Yes, yes, I know. I told the mayor we'd bring the video over and play it for him as soon as we close tonight."

Dad and I drove to the Callahan's house together. It was in the nicest area, just off the beach on the north side of town. Mayor and Mrs. Callahan owned an upscale women's clothing boutique in Cliffview. The two-story house was a tribute to how popular and successful it was.

Margo answered the door. While she was as immaculately dressed and groomed as usual she looked a couple of decades older. Mayor Callahan probably hadn't slept in days.

Conversation was minimal. The Callahans led us to a large family room just off the spacious kitchen and sat close together on the sofa, holding hands. Dad connected his laptop to the TV and clicked on the wedding video. He fast-forwarded through the rehearsal dinner and the short sequence of Linda Arneson demonstrating how pregnant she was.

Next up was the Bride's Room melee. Margo began weeping silently as she watched her daughter send her back to her condo for the third time.

"I was so impatient," she cried. "Why did I have to be so impatient?"

"You didn't know, Margo, you didn't know," the mayor said.

When the scenes of the wedding were shown, Margo wept openly.

"She was so beautiful. Everyone said they'd never seen such a beautiful bride."

Then it was time for the reception.

"You may not want to watch this," I said.

"No, no, we have to see it," the mayor insisted. "There may be something that will prove Veronica and Georgia had nothing to do with Cat's death."

By the time the cake feeding began, my stomach was in knots. It had been hard enough to experience the tragedy first hand. Seeing it happen again was excruciatingly painful. As we watched Chip carefully feed Cat the first small piece of cake, we heard Margo say, "Have some more, Cat. We want to make sure we get good photos."

Margo unraveled completely. "I killed my own daughter," she wailed. "I killed my own daughter."

Dad stopped the video and we all tried to tell her it wasn't her fault but she was distraught. The mayor called the family doctor. When Dad and I started to leave, he begged us to stay.

"Let me get Margo calmed down. Then I want to see the rest of the video."

The mayor led his wife upstairs. When the doctor came, he went upstairs, too. After the doctor left, the mayor returned to the family room.

"I'm sorry," I said. "I forgot Margo had asked Cat to eat more cake."

"It's not your fault. Let's get on with it, I want to see the rest."

There wasn't much more. We watched Cat dance with her dad and with Chip before she collapsed and died. As I was pushed out of the way the video jumped wildly around then ended abruptly.

I looked at the mayor. His face was white. He sat silently on the sofa for a few minutes.

"I didn't see anything that would help clear my sister, did you?"

Dad and I looked at each other and he answered for both of us. "No."

The mayor got to his feet like an old man.

"I appreciate you coming." He walked us to the door. We got in Dad's truck and drove off. We were silent until we parked in front of my condo.

As I started to get out Dad said: "Cinnamon, let's go to my house. I want to see part of that video again."

He refused to elaborate. At his house, he set up the laptop and started the video again, fast-forwarding through the footage of the rehearsal and the dinner that followed. Next we saw the women preparing the hall for the reception. I couldn't help smiling when Linda did her little dance. Dad stopped the video when the camera focused on the object she had stepped on.

"A BMW keyless remote? What did you do with it?"

I stared at him blankly. "I asked the women who were working in the hall if they knew whose it was. When no one claimed it, I put it in my purse."

"Do you still have it?"

I was mystified by his interest. I took my purse and upended it on the rug. I had a comb, a lipstick, a couple of paper clips, a small bottle of hand lotion, a Chapstick, one cough drop, a wallet, two tampons, a couple of facial tissues and the keys for my condo, van and Greene's, all on one ring. There was no BMW keyless remote.

"No other pockets it could be in?"

I emptied all of those, too. No keyless remote.

"What did you do with it?" Dad was persistent.

"I don't know. When I finished checking out the reception hall, I went to the Bride's Room. I don't remember doing anything with the remote."

"Let's look at the video again, starting with Linda," Dad suggested. "Maybe something will jog your memory."

He went back to Linda's finding of the remote and we watched it again. When we got to the part filmed in the Bride's Room, however, I heard one of the bridesmaids sneezing. Then she could clearly be heard wailing, "Omigod, I'm allergic to the flowers." More sneezing followed.

"Stop," I yelled.

Dad paused the video.

"Linda Arneson sent Jennifer to the Bride's Room with an antihistamine for the sneezing bridesmaid. I gave the car remote to her when she left and asked her to give it to her mother. Why is the remote so important?"

"It could belong to the murderer."

"There were hundreds of people there that day."

"True. And the remote could also belong to someone who had nothing whatsoever to do with Cat's death. But right now it is the only thing we've got."

I looked at my watch. "Should we call the Arnesons now?"

"Jennifer is probably asleep. I'll call early tomorrow and ask her dad if we can talk to her before she goes to school. Pick you up at 8:00?"

"Sure," I said.

I went right to bed when I got home.

Chapter 20

Pastor Arneson answered the door when we knocked. He looked tired.

"Come on in. Jennifer's in the kitchen having breakfast."

"How are Linda and the baby?" I asked.

"They're great, just great."

Jennifer was seated at the table in the kitchen eating a bowl of cereal. She brightened when she saw me.

"Cinnamon." she said. "Did you hear I have a brother? I got to see him in the window at the hospital but they wouldn't let me hold him. Mom says I'll have plenty of time to do that when they come home."

"That's wonderful," I said, sitting down in the chair next to her. "And I'm sure you'll be a big help, just like you were on the day of the wedding."

Jennifer grew solemn. "Cat was so beautiful. Are you going to her funeral?"

"I think everyone in town will be at the funeral. But my dad and I need to ask you something about the day Cat got married. Do you remember your mom asking you to take medicine for a bridesmaid's allergy to the church?"

"Sure. It was for Cassidy. She said the flowers made her sneeze."

"When you got there, do you remember my giving you something to give to your mother?"

Jennifer thought for a minute. "You gave me a car remote. It had BMW on it. You said you didn't know who lost it. The kids at school call BMWs 'Beamers.'"

"What did you do with the remote?"

"I gave it to my mom."

"And what did she do with it?"

Jennifer shrugged. "She was in her bedroom lying down. She had her eyes closed. I put the remote on her nightstand and told her what you said. She said, 'Thank you, sweetie,' and told me to get dressed for the wedding."

"Were you home, Pastor?" Dad asked.

"I'm sure I was already at the church."

Jennifer confirmed that. "Daddy went to the church before Mom sent me to the Bride's Room."

"So what did Linda do with the remote?" I asked.

"I don't remember seeing one around here," Arneson said. "Let's go look in the bedroom."

Dad and I left Jennifer eating her cereal and followed Pastor Arneson out of the kitchen and down a hall. We passed two bedrooms. One was obviously Jennifer's, the other the nursery. The Arnesons' bedroom was neat and the bed was made. Pastor Arneson checked the tops and drawers of the nightstands on either side of it as well as the tops of the two dressers. He knelt down and used a flashlight to look under all of the furniture, including the bed. He didn't find a car remote.

"Where might she have put it?" I asked.

"I have no idea," Arneson said.

We trooped back to the kitchen.

"Why is this remote is so important?"

"We're not sure," Dad said. "Linda found it just outside the back door of the reception hall after lunch. Cinnamon asked those in the kitchen and those in the hall about it but nobody claimed it."

"I also asked everyone in the Bride's Room," I remembered.

"Lots of people were in and out that day," Arneson pointed out.

"Yes, but if someone lost the remote to his or her car, how would they get home? Did anyone ask you if a remote had been found?"

"No. And I see your point," Arneson replied, looking thoughtful. "Was it on the sidewalk or in the grass?"

"In the grass. I was taking a video of Linda in all her pregnant splendor and she stepped on it."

"The gardener mowed the lawn Friday afternoon. If it had been there then, it probably would have been chewed up by the mower. So it must have been dropped after that.

"I'm going over to see my wife and baby at 10:30. Want to come? I can show off my son and you can ask Linda about the remote."

Dad looked at me. "I need to be in the store. Why don't you go, Cinnamon?"

"Okay. Which hospital?"

"Santa Barbara General. I can pick you up."

"Great," I said. "I'll be at the store. Just honk and I'll come out. Bye Jennifer. Have a good day at school."

"Bye," Jennifer replied. "You'll like the baby, he's really cute."

Dad and I went back to Greene's. Before I knew

it, it was 10:30 and Pastor Arneson was outside.

Danny's truck passed us as we drove out of town on Cliffview Boulevard. I waved at him, then realized he probably wouldn't know it was me in Pastor Arneson's SUV. On the way to Santa Barbara, Arneson and I chatted easily about the church, Jennifer, Linda and the new baby. We didn't discuss the wedding. Arneson did say, however, that Cat's funeral would be held Thursday afternoon. He said her body had been sent to Santa Barbara for autopsy and would be released to the mortuary after that was completed.

At the hospital we went directly to the maternity ward on the second floor. Linda was sitting up in bed, looking tired but exceedingly happy.

"I've got a surprise for you, Linda," Arneson told his wife as he bent over to hug and kiss her. "I've brought Cinnamon."

"You're a lot skinnier than you were the last time I saw you."

"I've lost 35 pounds, another 15 to go. Have you seen the baby yet? He's so beautiful. I just fed him."

"We came right to your room. I'll take her by the nursery when we leave. Actually, Cinnamon has a question for you."

"Remember the car remote we found outside the reception hall when I was filming you?"

Linda gave me a blank look.

"You stepped on it but you couldn't bend over to pick it up," I reminded her.

Her face cleared. "Oh yeah. You said you'd ask around and see if you could find out who owned it."

"When Jennifer brought the antihistamine to the

Bride's Room, I gave the remote to her. She told us you were lying down and she left it on one of the nightstands."

Linda frowned. "I was having contractions and not paying much attention to anything else. I was worried I'd deliver during the wedding. I remember Jennifer coming back. I don't remember her mentioning a remote."

"Linda called a taxi to take her to the hospital right after the wedding," Pastor Arneson said. "I didn't even know she was gone till much later. I got here just before the baby was born."

"You had your hands full," Linda said.

She turned to me. "I get home, I'll try to remember what I did with the remote and look for it then. Is it important?"

"It could be," I said.

On the way out we stopped at the nursery and Don Arneson pointed out his son. Recognizing the pastor, a nurse picked up the baby and brought him close to the window so we could get a better look. Arneson beamed.

"I was surprised he's so big," he told me. "Jennifer only weighed seven pounds."

"I think he looks just like you," I said.

Arneson's smile widened. "That's what Linda says, too. Did I tell you we've named him Lucas? That's my middle name."

We drove back to Cliffview, once again discussing everything but the wedding. As we got close to town, I said: "Do many members of your congregation own BMWs?"

"I know there's a few," he said, then added,

"While Linda has an excellent memory she's going to be very busy. We'll just have to hope she remembers something. I'll keep an eye out for the remote and ask Jennifer to do the same."

He dropped me off in front of Greene's. Inside the store, Dad told me Danny had called. I called him but the person who answered the phone said he'd gone to lunch.

Danny called back late in the afternoon. He said he'd pick me up at 6:00 the next morning and would bring the gear I had rented the previous Wednesday.

"We're still on for dinner tomorrow night, right?" he asked.

"Of course. What sort of woman do you think I am? One who sleeps through dates or cancels them?"

"Now why would I think that?"

I picked up dinner and a scuba diving magazine at the supermarket on the way home. I went to bed early, because I had to get up early. For once, things worked out the way I expected.

Chapter 21

I'd packed my stuff the night before and set it beside the front door. Danny was bringing coffee and bagels. But I still had to roll out of my sleeping bag and get dressed, a monumental task for me at 5:30 am. I was brushing my teeth when the doorbell rang.

"Sunshine. You're up. Are you ready to go?" Danny looked as if he had been up for hours and was loveing every minute.

"Just a sec," I mumbled, remembering I had not combed my hair. By the time I presented myself at the front door again, my bag had been carted away and Danny was standing in the doorway, grinning.

There was no traffic and the trip to Santa Barbara Harbor took about 10 minutes. Soon we were carting our gear to the *California Diver*. Dad and Sandy had gotten there just before us. Many of the passengers gathered in the galley to have breakfast. Others went below to sleep during the two-hour cruise to Santa Cruz Island.

Danny and I did, too. The bunkroom was one of the best ones I'd seen on a California dive boat. It opened onto the stern deck with a broad flight of stairs. Bunks stacked two high lined the sides; bunks stacked three high formed an island in the middle. Ours was a lower bunk on the port side. Danny slid in first and I followed, pulling the curtains closed. The bunks had pillows and blankets. Danny had already spread one blanket over the vinyl mattress, now he covered us with another. I snuggled up close to him, my back against his chest. He put his arms around me and pulled me near. It felt good to lie next to him. He kissed my neck and whispered in my ear, "Sleep tight, Sunshine." The gentle rocking of the boat and the muffled roar of its diesels lulled me to sleep even though every pore in my body tingled at being so close to Danny.

It seemed hardly any time at all had passed before I heard the engines slow and Danny say, "Time to dive, Sunshine." He climbed over me and out of the bunk, closing the curtains behind him. I stretched and considered sleeping in. Since it was lobster season, however, I decided I'd better get up. I rolled out of the bunk and went topside.

The deck was bustling with activity. Sandy and Dad were already in their wetsuits and Danny was pulling on his. Paul and Pete were slipping into buoyancy compensators and tanks while other divers were already fully geared up and standing on the port side of the deck near the bow. I began getting into my wetsuit.

The sun was hidden by the thick overcast. It was breezy and a little choppy; the boat crew was having trouble anchoring. I was dressed and ready to go several minutes before the captain announced the gates were open and we could dive.

The giant stride off the bow of the *California Diver* is not my favorite water entry. It's about an eight foot drop and seems much longer. Because there was a current, the captain had opened only the bow gate. He advised us to swim quickly to the anchor line and descend along it so we wouldn't be swept away.

The divers jumped in, one by one. Finally, it was my turn.

The water was cold, only 56°F. I didn't have time to think about it because it took some strenuous kicking to reach the anchor line. I followed Danny down it hand over hand. At about 50 feet the current dissipated. We let go of the line and kicked to the bottom at 70 feet before heading off to look for lobsters. Visibility was only about 20 feet and, since we were so deep, it was dark. We wandered through the kelp, looking for places lobsters might live. It was a good 15 minutes before we came across a rocky crevice in which three sets of antennae bristled. Danny quickly grabbed one lobster and bagged it then reached for another. The third bug panicked, jetting backward through the water over Danny's shoulder. When it landed on the bottom, I pounced on it, pinning it to the sand.

By the time we bagged that lobster it was time to return to the boat. We retraced our route before surfacing behind the boat and letting the current carry us to it.

The sun never did come out that day and we spent our surface intervals in the galley, sipping hot liquids with Dad, Sandy, Paul and Pete. Danny and I made two more dives without bagging a single bug. Sandy and Dad didn't get any all day. Paul got two and Pete had a grand total of one.

Most divers went down below to nap on the boat ride home but the six of us remained in the galley talking.

"Georgia and Veronica couldn't kill anyone," Danny said, voicing all our sentiments. "I wish we could do something to help them."

"Tell them about the keyless remote, Cinnamon," Dad prompted.

I related the story while everyone listened.

"With a new baby Linda isn't going to have time to look for the remote," Sandy said. "Meanwhile, Veronica and Georgia could be charged with murder at any time. I think the cops are ignoring any evidence that doesn't point to them."

Dad said: "Veronica has retained Andrew Abogado, a Santa Barbara lawyer. I called him last night to tell him about the remote. He said ground peanuts were found in the top layer of the cake. Everyone in town knows Cat is allergic to peanuts, she nearly died when she accidentally ate a brownie containing them in high school."

Dad turned to Paul. "Remember the article you ran on the cake? It said Veronica would bake the layers in the reception hall kitchen and Georgia would assemble and decorate them the next day.

"Georgia told Abogado that when she started putting the cake together she noticed the top layer looked different. She would have asked Veronica about that but couldn't reach her.

"Veronica says that other than their size, the layers she baked were identical. All that is left of the cake is the anniversary layer, which was wrapped, put in a box designed for freezer storage and refrigerated right after Chip and Cat finished with it. Guests apparently didn't realize there was any problem with the cake and demolished the rest of it. Many of those who left through the kitchen grabbed pieces to take with them when they were asked to leave the hall after Cat collapsed."

"Was the anniversary layer box fingerprinted?" I asked.

"No. The one the cake is in now wasn't the original, which was probably thrown away."

"So someone substituted a layer with peanuts in it for the original layer," I said. "It would have been easy to do. A lot of people were in and out of the reception hall when the cake layers were sitting on the kitchen counter in The Bakery's pink boxes."

"I agree," Dad said. "However, I don't think the murderer would have risked making the exchange when there were people around who might see him or her. I'd bet it was done when the hall was unoccupied."

"There are apartments and condos along the two streets before you get to the church," I said. "If somebody was doing something they didn't want anyone to know about they'd probably park their car on the street rather than in the church lot, where the Arnesons or someone else might see it."

"Good point." Danny said. "The remote you found was from a BMW. How do we find out if a BMW was parked where it shouldn't have been?"

"Maybe we could post fliers in apartment and condo buildings asking if anyone saw anything out of the ordinary on the night before the wedding or the next morning," I suggested.

"That's a terrific idea," Dad said. He sounded excited. "Parking is not allowed on most of the streets close to the beach without a special permit. Maybe someone will remember an illegally parked BMW. We can make the fliers at the store tonight and post them in the buildings tomorrow after work."

"We can post them on the street lights, too," I said.

Paul, who had been listening carefully while stroking his beard, had an idea. "I've felt from the get-go that Lawson was barking up the wrong tree by focusing on Veronica and Georgia. I've been thinking of running an editorial about that. I'll write one tomorrow and send our photographer to The Bakery to take a photo of Veronica and Georgia to go with it. Maybe that will get Lawson moving in the right direction."

We all thought that was a great idea.

"I'll run a copy of the flier next to my editorial," Paul said. "We'll deliver a one, two punch. The fliers will be distributed tomorrow evening and the editorial will run in the paper the next day. Maybe we'll flush a murderer out of hiding."

California Diver was entering the harbor by then and it was time to get our gear together and get off the boat. Twenty minutes later, Danny and I were in his truck, headed south to Cliffview. Dad and Sandy were just ahead of us, Paul and Pete a few cars behind.

"I want to help Veronica and Georgia," Danny said, reaching over for my hand, "but I'm beginning to think I'm never going to be alone with you when you're awake."

"We can go to your place when we finish the fliers tonight."

"I have to drop my gear at my store first. You can leave yours there, too, if you like. I've got a big rinse tank and plenty of storage room. You won't have to use your bathtub."

"I'd love that. My bathroom isn't very big and I'd prefer not to dry my gear on the balcony.

"By the way, are you going to Cat's funeral?"

Danny shook his head. "No. I expect most of the town will be there though. A lot of businesses will be closed for several hours."

"Sandy isn't going either. Since Dad and I will be at the service and the Callahans' house after it, Greene's will be closed all afternoon."

We rode the next couple of miles in silence, following Dad and Sandy when they turned off at Cliffview Avenue and drove into the mall.

Inside the photo store, we quickly agreed that food came first. Sandy wrote down our dinner orders, phoned them into Juanita's and went to pick them up. Meanwhile, Pete, Paul, Danny, Dad and I gathered around the computer in Dad's office. We finally composed the following:

"PLEASE HELP"

"Last Friday evening or Saturday morning you may have seen a vehicle parked illegally in a restricted parking zone. This vehicle may have been used to commit a very serious crime. If you saw such a vehicle or noticed anything unusual please call 444-4466."

When everyone agreed the flier looked good, we sat around the conference table in Dad's office and ate our dinners. Then we made 300 copies of the flier and divided them into three piles. Our target area consisted of six blocks; with the three of us working we thought it would take a couple of hours at the most.

When the fliers were printed and everyone had a stack of them, Danny and I drove to his shop. He parked his truck in the back and unlocked the door to a big room with a concrete floor. There was a large stainless steel tank full of freshwater in the middle of it. We dumped all of our gear in the tank, rinsed it thoroughly and hung it up to dry on the PVC racks that lined the walls.

By the time we were finished, it was nearly 10:00 pm and I was beginning to fade. I stifled a yawn as we got ready to leave. Danny put his arms around me.

"Why do I think you'd sleep through another date if I took you home with me? Is it because your eyes are already at half mast?"

"Sorry, Danny. I'm really tired. I should have napped on the boat on the way home."

"I've got a class tomorrow night," Danny said, "and I pick up Sam on Friday afternoon. Want to have dinner with us Friday night and watch a video? I should warn you that Sam gets to choose the video."

"I'll probably love what he chooses," I said. "Maybe I'll even be able stay awake."

Danny pulled me closer and kissed me a long time. He made it very difficult to stop. We finally pulled apart and left the store, driving to my condo in silence. He walked me to my door and kissed me again, briefly this time.

"See you Friday night, Sunshine," he said as he left.

I showered and slipped into my sleeping bag. Getting up early, making three dives and all that fresh salt air took their toll. I fell asleep almost as soon as my head touched my pillow.

Chapter 22

Thursday morning was slow at Greene's. The whole town was preparing for Cat Callahan Forester's funeral, to be held at the church where she was married and died.

Dad and I were anxious for the day to pass quickly. We wanted to post our fliers.

About 10:00 am I called Linda Arneson, hoping to jog her memory about the BMW remote. As the phone was ringing, I remembered that mother and baby had only been home a short time and that Pastor Arneson would be preparing for the funeral. I was about to hang up when a woman answered. It wasn't Linda.

"Hello, may I speak to Linda?" I could hear a baby wailing in the background.

"I'm sorry," a woman said, "she's trying to feed her son at the moment. I'm Linda's mom, can I take a message?"

"This is Cinnamon Greene. I was hoping Linda had remembered what she did with the car remote we found the day of the wedding. Can you mention it to her? I'll call back in a day or two."

The wailing stopped and there was a pause. "She did it," Linda's mom said. "The baby is nursing."

"Congratulate her for me," I said dryly.

"Will do. Now, what did you want?"

I repeated my message, thanked Linda's mom

and hung up. Somehow I doubted Linda would have time to think about the remote for several years.

Cat's service was supposed to start at 3:00. We closed the store at 1:00 and set off for the church. Normally, we would have arrived way before the crowds. Not today. We got one of the last spaces in the parking lot and only just managed to squeeze into the last two spots in the last pew.

Arneson had made sure the church was prepared for the crowds. Those who couldn't get into the church could watch the service on closed-circuit TV in the reception hall, where folding chairs and two large screen TVs had been set up.

The elaborate casket that sat before the altar was closed and covered with flowers. During the service, many people wept. When he tried to deliver the eulogy Chip broke down completely. The maid of honor stepped in to finish it and a couple of the bridesmaids gave tributes. Mayor Callahan, his face drawn and white, said a few words about his daughter and thanked the town for its support.

The reception at the Callahan house was by invitation only and considerably smaller. The mayor, Mrs. Callahan and Chip were so mired in grief they were barely functional.

While I had barely known Cat and hadn't felt anything at all when she died, my heart ached for those she left behind. Their lives had changed forever. "Everyone should go home and leave these people alone," I said.

Since Dad felt the same way we didn't stay long.

At home later, I changed into comfortable clothes, grabbed my set of fliers and set out for the area assigned to me.

It was almost impossible to find a place to park that wouldn't result in a ticket. I finally ended up several blocks away. Posting the fliers took less time than I expected.

I had agreed to meet Dad and Sandy for dinner at Cliffview's new vegetarian restaurant, Simply Natural. Sandy had had lunch there a few days before and thought we'd like it.

Dad and I ordered what Sandy recommended, a veggie burger on a whole wheat bun with avocado and cheese. It came with a small green salad. When our bottle of wine came, we toasted our efforts on Veronica and Georgia's behalf.

After inhaling our food in record time, we sat sipping what remained of the wine.

"I know several people in town who drive BMWs," Sandy said, "including Jason and Megan."

"Both hated Cat," I noted. "If either of them lives near the church, however, he or she wouldn't have to park illegally to leave a doctored cake layer in its kitchen."

Sandy said: "Jason lives in Santa Barbara. Megan has an apartment just behind the mall. She leaves her car behind her shop because she doesn't have a parking space where she lives."

Then she added: "While Jason isn't a very nice person, I can't believe he'd kill anyone. Ditto Megan."

I said, "We really need to find that remote. I think it's the key, no pun intended, to this whole mess."

Dad and Sandy nodded agreement.

We left Simply Natural about 9:30. Dad and Sandy dropped me off in front of my condo before heading back to her place. I showered and rolled into my sleeping bag. It occurred to me that I should shop for a bed sometime soon because sleeping on the floor was getting old. I managed to read four chapters of the Sue Grafton novel before dropping off to sleep.

Chapter 23

Friday morning dawned bright and warm. Or was it was just the thought of spending the evening with Danny that made me feel such a glow? The unknown was his son. What if we didn't get along? It was more than a little important that we did.

I walked to Greene's, stopping at The Bakery. Although it had been closed just one morning since Cat died, Veronica and Georgia were clearly struggling. The inventory of baked goods was shockingly low and there was no vanilla bean coffee. Still, I took it as a good sign that it was open at all. I bought coffee and a bran muffin to go. While I didn't see Georgia, her mother appeared extremely distressed.

At Greene's, Dad had several copies of the Chronicle, hand delivered by its publisher. The editorial proclaiming Veronica and Georgia's innocence and a copy of our flier was on the front page. A photo of Veronica and Georgia behind the counter of The Bakery illustrated it. They looked as if the world was about to end.

Greene's voice and e-mail messages were already clogged with responses to our fliers and the newspaper story and our phones rang continuously. Unfortunately, few of the callers had anything of any value to tell us. They were hoping we would tell them what we knew and/or just wanted to express support for our project.

Chief Lawson showed up about 10:00 am. He was not happy. He told us he had already expressed his disapproval of the article and flier to the Chronicle's publisher. We all went into Dad's office, where, in a scene that could have been taken from a bad movie, Lawson demanded to know what we thought we were doing. The conversation would have been comical if the subject wasn't so serious.

"I don't appreciate amateurs taking the law into their own hands," he grumbled. "You guys don't know all the facts. You have no idea what you're doing. You've opened a can of worms with that damn flier."

"You've gone after the wrong people, Chief," I said. "Since you don't seem interested in finding out who really killed Cat, we've been forced to do your job for you."

"Interfere with my investigation and you'll live to regret it," Lawson growled.

"What investigation?" I asked. "Everyone in town thinks Veronica and Georgia are innocent. Yet you've focused on them and aren't doing anything to find the real killer."

Hands on hips, I glowered at the chief. Lawson glowered back.

"I'm warning you," he said. "Stay out of it. You get any information from those fliers or that editorial, you contact me immediately." Then he stalked off. A few minutes later Dad got a phone call telling us the police were riding around town and tearing down all our fliers.

We hoped they were too late and that between the fliers and the editorial someone who knew something of value would be contacting us soon. And, they did. Among the hundreds of phone calls we got that day were five that buoyed our spirits. All of them concerned cars parked illegally on the night in question. Three of the callers, permit holders who had been unable to find spaces near their apartments because of illegally parked cars, had reported them to the police. Two had written down the license plate numbers and makes of the cars and kept the information, pointing out that some people routinely parked illegally.

One of the cars was a black BMW. Dad called Sandy and asked if she could find out what Jason's license plate numbers were. Sandy said she'd see if his car was in its usual space next to his office and call Dad back. I walked to Megan's salon to check out her car, which was parked in the alley behind it. However, neither the car's color (it was slate blue) nor its personalized license plates (Megan HnN) matched those our caller had given us. By the time I got back to Greene's, Sandy had called to say Jason was out of town. We'd have to wait until Monday to check his plates.

Dad and I were elated. Neither of us liked Jason. We were sure his license plates would match those on the illegally parked BMW. It was frustrating to have to wait till Monday to confirm our suspicions. We thought about telling Chief Lawson about it and decided against it. We thought it would be better to have the case neatly tied up before telling him anything. Besides, nothing would happen until Jason returned.

The numerous incoming phone calls on a usually

busy Friday made the day pass quickly. After we closed the store, Dad dropped me off at my condo. He and Sandy were having dinner with friends in Camarillo.

At my condo, I showered and got ready for my date with Danny and Sam. I fussed about it for a few minutes before deciding to pack a small overnight bag. Would Danny want me to stay over with his son there? I had never dated anyone with kids before. I finally decided to pack a bag and leave it in my van. It would be there if I needed it, but if I didn't, no one would ever have to know about it.

I parked in front of Danny's house and walked up to it with a little apprehension. I pressed the doorbell. The door was flung open a few minutes later. A juvenile version of Danny stood in the doorway eyeing me.

"You've got red hair so you must be Cinnamon."

"And you look just like Danny, so you must be Sam. Nice to meet you."

I offered my hand and Sam shook it solemnly. Then he grinned. "Dad's in the backyard. Come on in."

He closed the door behind me and led the way through the living room and kitchen to the backyard. Clouds of smoke came from the grill that Danny hovered over. When the smoke cleared momentarily I saw what I thought were chicken halves. Danny didn't notice us at first, he was concentrating on the task at hand. His face was flushed and perspiration beaded his forehead. When he finally looked up, he smiled, then came over and kissed me on the cheek.

"Hi, Sunshine, dinner will be ready in about 20

minutes. There's beer in the fridge. Would you mind fixing a salad? Sam can show you where everything is and tell you what he likes in it."

"Why does he call you Sunshine?" Sam asked as we walked back inside.

"It's a joke. He calls me that because I'm not sunshiny when I wake up in the morning."

Sam nodded wisely. "The beer's in there," he said, pointing to the refrigerator. "I'll get the salad bowl."

The beer wasn't hard to find. Danny's refrigerator was just a little better supplied than my own. While I retrieved and opened a beer, Sam went into the tiny dining room and opened a cupboard. He came back with a large wooden bowl.

"I like lettuce, tomato, avocado and celery in my salad," he said. "No carrots."

I opened the fridge and took out the required items. From the opposite side of the small island in the middle of the kitchen Sam directed the activity, telling me where to find the knife, the cutting board and the salad dressing.

Clouds of smoke continued to puff from the backyard. When I finished the salad, Sam and I watched Danny laboring over the grill through the window over the sink.

"Are we having chicken? I thought he'd be serving lobster tonight," I said.

"I like lobsters, too, and Dad is really good at cooking them," Sam told me. "Can you cook?"

"Not really. I eat a lot of take-out."

"Dad has been trying to learn how to cook stuff other than lobsters for a while but I don't think he's ever going to get the hang of it. He makes good breakfasts, though. Sometimes we have Eggos waffles." He looked at me and grinned. It was impossible not to grin back.

"I was pretty good at catching lobsters years ago," I said. "Can't say I like cleaning and cooking them."

"What did your biggest one weigh?"

"Eight pounds."

"Wow. Do you have any pictures of it?"

"My dad has some. I'll bring them to show you next time."

"My mom doesn't dive, she's afraid of the water."

Just then Danny waved frantically from the backyard.

"He wants us to bring him the platter," Sam told me. "The chicken must be done."

We took the platter out to Danny, who loaded it with three well-charcoaled chicken halves. Sam and I took the platter inside as Danny put the lid on the grill and removed his apron.

Sam showed me where to put the platter and where to sit. Danny joined us.

"The skin's a little burned," he observed. "If you take it off, the chicken should be fine." He used tongs to put chicken halves on both my plate and Sam's.

"I can't eat all of this," I said.

"That's okay," Sam said quickly. "We'll give you a doggie bag."

I soon understood why he wanted to give the chicken away. Although I removed the burnt skin my first bite indicated it wasn't the only part of the bird that was overcooked.

Danny didn't seem to notice. He ate his half quickly. "It's a little dry," he said, in the understatement of the day. "Is that all you're going to eat, Cinnamon?"

"I had a big, late lunch," I lied. As a matter of fact, I couldn't remember eating lunch and probably hadn't. "Why don't you take some of mine?"

"Want more, Sam?"

"I've got plenty, Dad," Sam replied. He and I ate a lot of salad while Danny worked his way through the well-grilled poultry.

When we finished, Danny and Sam cleared the table, insisting I stay put.

"We've got cookie dough ice cream for dessert," Sam announced. "It's my favorite."

Each of us ate two scoops of that. Afterward, we helped Danny load the dishwasher and clean up the kitchen before moving to the living room. While I relaxed with a cup of coffee, Danny and Sam disappeared into his son's bedroom. After Sam took a shower and got ready for bed, we'd watch the Disney video he'd chosen.

Sam came bounding into the living room about 15 minutes later and hopped up on the sofa next to me. He was pajama clad and freshly scrubbed. His hair was still wet. Danny followed him with a towel and comb. He dried his son's hair and combed it. Since it was just as curly as his own, the comb job rapidly came undone. While Sam was returning the towel and comb to the bathroom, Danny said, "Hope you like *Finding Nemo*. We've seen it numerous times."

"I'm sure I'll love it."

Sam returned and wedged himself up against his dad's right side. I sat on Danny's left. He put an arm around each of us. The movie played. I enjoyed it and didn't fall asleep.

When it was over, Danny took Sam off to bed. As he left the living room he said, "Good night, Cinnamon. Are you sleeping over?"

I turned bright red. "I don't know," I said. Danny was no help, he was busy grinning that wicked grin of his.

"Well, then, maybe I'll see you in the morning," Sam said. "We have to get up early because Dad has a beach class. I'm going with him. She can come, too, can't she?"

"Sunshine isn't much of a morning person, Sam," Danny told him. "It's highly unlikely she'll want to get up at 7:00. And I think she has to work tomorrow."

"Your dad is right. You don't want to see me that early. And I do have to work, so I can't go to the beach with you."

A few minutes later, Danny sat down next to me.

"I saw the editorial in the newspaper. Paul did a great job. Did you get any responses from it and the fliers?"

I told him about all the calls, our confrontation with Chief Lawson and our suspicions about Jason. Danny bristled when I told him about the chief's grandstanding but didn't seem to share Dad's and my conviction that Jason had murdered Cat.

"What if his plates don't match?"

I really hadn't considered that. "I don't know," I

admitted. "They've got to be his."

"But what if they're not?" he persisted.

I shrugged. "Guess we'll cross that bridge when we get to it." For the first time a little doubt crept in. Maybe Jason wasn't the killer.

"You probably should have told Lawson. He can look up license plates instantly."

I hated to admit that none of us had thought of that. "Jason is gone for the weekend. Lawson would have to wait till he comes home to arrest him anyway."

"I wonder if there's some way to trace the remote," Danny said. "Provided, of course, that Linda finds it."

"I don't know," I said. "Maybe I should visit a BMW dealer and find out everything I can about their remotes."

We were silent a few minutes before Danny asked, "What do you think of Sam?"

"He's a great kid and boy, does he look like you. His grin isn't as wicked as yours but it will be in time."

"He likes you," Danny said.

I was pleased. "Well, I like him, too."

Danny put his arms around me and pulled me close. The next kiss we shared left me breathless.

That's when the phone rang, startling both of us. We sat bolt upright. My heart was pounding. A phone call at this time of night is never good. Danny found his smart phone and picked it up after the third ring. He said "Hello," listened a minute, then handed the phone to me.

"It's Lawson."

"What's wrong? Is my dad okay?"

"Take it easy, Cinnamon," Chief Lawson said. "No one's been hurt. Someone threw a Molotov cocktail at your store. Luckily, the bottle didn't go through the window, it bounced off and broke on the sidewalk. There doesn't seem to be any damage to your store. But someone should come over here and take a look at it. Since Red isn't answering his cell, we called you."

"I'll be there in a few minutes," I said, wondering how the hell Lawson knew where *I* was.

Danny wanted to grab Sam and come with me. I told him no. "I'll call you as soon as I can. Chief Lawson said there was no damage and I'll bet all of the town's police and firemen are there."

I was almost right. Most of Cliffview's police cars and one of its fire engines sat in the parking lot in front of Greene's, all of them with lights flashing. A sizable crowd had gathered. I had to park in front of the home improvement center and push my way through to our store, where Chief Lawson, four police officers and three firemen stood laughing and chatting with the security guard who had answered our burglar alarm and turned it off. He said the store was locked when he got there and it didn't look as if anyone had gotten inside.

I said, "Chief, can you ask your men to turn off their flashing lights? I don't think we need to attract more people. The whole town seems to be here already."

Chief Lawson glared at me before issuing an order. In a few minutes the lights ceased flashing.

"You were very lucky," Lawson said. "The

janitorial crew at Juanita's just happened to be leaving the restaurant when the cocktail was thrown. They grabbed fire extinguishers, ran down here and put out the fire. Unfortunately, they didn't see who threw the cocktail."

The sidewalk in front of the store was covered with a smelly, messy mixture of fire extinguisher foam and gasoline. I thanked the two men who had put out the fire before unlocking the door and turning on the lights. Chief Lawson and I walked through the store, noting that nothing had been disturbed. Three of Greene's employees showed up while we were doing that and a fourth arrived shortly thereafter.

Outside, the sidewalk was being cleaned.

Chief Lawson, the staff and I were discussing what had happened when Dad joined us. He was out of breath and very pale.

"Sandy and I were on our way home when we saw the crowd. Are you all right? What happened?"

"I'm fine, Dad. I wasn't here when someone tried to set our store on fire."

Chief Lawson and I told him what happened. Then he asked the question that had been on my mind since I heard about the fire.

"Do you suppose Paul's editorial and our fliers touched a nerve?"

"That would be my guess. Someone doesn't want us finding out something."

"Hold on, now," Chief Lawson said. "This is probably nothing more than a teenage prank."

Dad and I turned to look at him. "So this happens all the time in Cliffview?" I asked.

"Well, no. But that doesn't mean anything. It

could be the first of many. These kinds of things happen in other places."

"Right," Dad and I said simultaneously, our voices dripping with disgust.

Just then Sandy ran up. She had dropped Dad off before parking her car. We told her what had happened and she said, "It looks like someone didn't like our fliers."

Chief Lawson threw up his hands and walked off. After he conferred with his officers, the police cars and fire engine left. The crowd began to disperse.

I called Danny as soon as I got home. I told him everything that had happened, including Sandy's, Dad's and my belief the fliers and editorial were behind the attack on the store.

"That's what I've been thinking since you left. I don't think you're safe at your condo. Maybe you should stay with me until this whole thing is over."

"The attack tonight was amateurish," I said. "The bottle didn't even go through the window. I think someone's just trying to scare us."

I believed what I said when I said it. Later, in the dark of night, I began to feel less secure. The store had been attacked when no one would be there. But someone had already been killed. Would there be another incident and another victim? My mind whirled with possibilities and I didn't fall into an uneasy sleep until the sky began to lighten in the east.

Chapter 24

A furious Jilted Lover had ripped down and destroyed three fliers. The rampage would have continued if the risk of being seen wasn't so great.

Jilted Lover had no idea what the Greenes knew or what they were trying to find out. Whatever it was, however, it couldn't be good. Maybe someone had seen Jilted Lover's car parked on the street the night before the wedding and recognized it. Maybe someone had seen Jilted Lover on the morning of the murder. Maybe someone had found that damn remote and was trying to match it to a car. Maybe the fliers were intended to confirm or collect more information on all three.

Thinking about the possibilities had given Jilted Lover a headache. Something had to be done. The Greenes must be stopped. It shouldn't be hard. Neither one of them seemed like a fighter.

That is why Jilted Lover had targeted the Greenes' pride and joy, their camera store. If their livelihood was eliminated maybe they'd forget all about Cat Callahan Forester's untimely end.

While Jilted Lover had never set fire to anything other than gas logs in a fireplace the recipe for a Molotov cocktail was easy to find online and the ingredients readily available. It simply involved filling an empty wine bottle with gasoline and sticking a rag in the neck to act as a wick.

Jilted Lover waited until late Friday night, when

the mall was deserted, to do the deed. Wearing a black watch cap, sweatpants and sweatshirt, Jilted Lover had used the passage that led from the alley to the mall to walk casually toward the camera store. No one was around to see Jilted Lover light the rag, throw the bottle and melt into the darkness.

Unfortunately, the bottle hadn't been thrown hard enough. It triggered the store's burglar alarm when it bounced off a window then shattered harmlessly on the sidewalk. The volatile contents caught fire immediately. Returning to the scene in different clothes a few minutes later, Jilted Lover had been dismayed to see the store undamaged and two men putting out a small blaze with fire extinguishers.

This was my first time, Jilted Lover had thought. The next time I'll do better. Only the next time it won't be the store. The police will probably be watching it and that would be too dangerous for me. No, next time it will be your condo, Cinnamon dear.

Chapter 25

When I awoke at 9:30 am, my eyes felt as if they had sand in them and I had a horrible headache. Needless to say, I was even less sunshiny than usual. When I was leaving for work, I found an envelope addressed to me on the floor in front of my door. The note inside read: "Want to go out for pizza with us tonight? We'll pick you up about 5:30. I take Sam to his mother's afterward. Danny and Sam."

When I got near Greene's I saw a small crowd milling around outside, which meant it was packed with people inside. Half a block away, I detoured to the alley and entered through the back door. I went right to Dad's office and he closed the door behind me.

Before I could say anything he blurted out: "Georgia is gone."

I couldn't be hearing him right. "Georgia gone? Where?"

"No one knows. Veronica last saw her before she went to bed Thursday night. She was gone Friday morning. Veronica reported her missing about an hour ago. The Bakery is closed until further notice."

While I was trying to process this incomprehensible information, he added: "Until now, Veronica and Georgia had never spent a night apart."

"How did you find out?"

"Sandy called me. She heard it from the woman in her office who's dating a CPD officer. The police are trying to keep it quiet while they check it out. They are at Veronica's house right now."

"Good luck keeping it quiet. I'll bet half of Cliffview already knows."

"Why do you think I'm hiding in here?"

"I don't think I can handle this. Not today."

After taking a good look at me, Dad insisted I go home and get some sleep. I snuck out the back door and jogged home. Once there, however, I felt hyper. I did a couple of loads of laundry, made a sandwich and heated some soup for lunch, all while trying to figure out where Georgia had gone and why. She and her mother appeared to have a loving relationship and got along unusually well. I had never heard them exchange a harsh word. Surely wherever Georgia was she hadn't gone willingly. That thought was very troublesome.

After lunch I called the parsonage. Pastor Arneson answered. He sounded a bit harried. Although he already knew about the editorial, the fliers and the Molotov cocktail, he was eager to hear a first hand account. I said, "I was hoping to talk to Linda about the car remote. Do you think I could come over now? I could tell you everything that's happened then."

"Hang on a minute," he said. He muffled the phone with his hand and I could hear an indistinct conversation, then he was back. "Linda would love to see you. She says 3:00 pm would be good. Lucas usually naps for an hour after his afternoon feeding. We should have time to talk before he wakes up."

"Great," I said, "see you all then."

There was a children's store on Cliffview

Avenue a couple of blocks away. I walked over there and, with the help of a saleswoman, picked out gifts for Lucas and Jennifer. The store wrapped them for me and even added gift cards. I was able to get away with only a minimal discussion of the town's hottest topics. At my condo, I took an hour's nap, after which I felt much better.

Just before the appointed time, I drove over to the church. Jennifer answered the door. She was surprised to get a present.

"What's this for?"

"For helping your mom with the baby. How is he doing?"

"He's really cute even though all he does is sleep, eat, poop and cry. He's especially good at pooping."

Pastor Arneson strode down the hall toward us. "Cinnamon. Good to see you."

He led us to the kitchen/family room. Linda was sitting on the sofa, folding a heap of tiny, newly dried clothes. She looked tired but happy. Pastor Arneson introduced me to Linda's mother, Pam, a lively and petite senior citizen. She was loading the dishwasher in the kitchen.

I handed Linda the baby gifts.

"She gave me one, too," Jennifer told her. "Can I open it?"

"Sure sweetie," Linda said. Both she and her daughter opened the gifts. Jennifer was thrilled with her book and Linda was delighted with the little denim overalls and matching shirt I'd bought the baby.

"These are adorable. I can hardly wait for Lucas

to get big enough to wear them." After a few minutes, Linda suggested Jennifer take her new book to her room, telling her the adults needed to have a private conversation. Pam, meanwhile, was brewing a fresh pot of coffee and arranging cookies on a plate in the kitchen. She handed Jennifer a cookie wrapped in a napkin as the little girl left the room.

I told the Arnesons why we'd posted the fliers and why Paul Patterson had written his editorial. Then I told them about the attack on Greene's.

"Now you know why finding that car remote is so important," I said.

Linda looked thoughtful. "I just can't remember where it is," she said. "I was so stressed out about the contractions I could hardly think of anything else."

"Maybe we should reenact that day," I suggested.

"I'm willing to try anything," Linda said. She and I went down the hall to the Arneson's bedroom. Linda lay down on the bed. "You'll have to keep an eye on me," she said. "I'm likely to nod off."

She lay there a few minutes with her eyes closed. Just when I thought she had fallen asleep, she frowned and said: "As soon as I lay down, I realized I was having contractions. I worried my water would break and the baby would be born during the wedding.

"I remember the call from the Bride's Room about the sneezing bridesmaid. I got up, found a package of antihistamines and asked Jennifer to take them to the church. I was still lying here when she returned. She came in, put the remote in my hand and told me you hadn't been able to find its owner.

"I slept for about 20 minutes. When I awoke the

remote was still in my hand. I put it in my purse and got dressed for the wedding. Jennifer and I walked over to Don's office. I wanted to tell him about the contractions but he was already gone. His secretary was just leaving her office...." Linda opened her eyes and sat up abruptly. She clapped her hands.

"That's it. I remember what I did with it." Her face showed relief.

"I gave the remote to our church secretary, Caroline Walker. I asked her to put it in the lost and found."

"Wonderful. Can we go get it now?"

We went back to the family room and shared our news with Pastor Arneson and Linda's mom. Pastor was on his feet immediately. "I can take you there now if you'd like."

We were out of the house and walking rapidly toward the church almost before the words were out of his mouth. I had to trot to keep up with him. His secretary's office was right next to his. He unlocked the door and we stepped inside. It was small and tidy. Mrs. Walker, I decided, was probably very efficient.

Pastor Arneson went immediately to the cupboard where the lost and found items were kept. He pulled out a box and upended it on the rug. Squatting on the floor, we sorted through the items. Our excitement, at a fever pitch when we walked in, slowly ebbed. There was a child's blue sweater; a Dodgers baseball cap; a little girl's pink stocking; a boy's green jacket; a small stainless steel bowl; a wooden spoon; a bald Barbie; and a maroon tie. There were no keyless remotes. One by one Arneson picked up the items and put them back in the box. He shook the clothing to make sure the pockets were empty.

When he finished, we got slowly to our feet. Pastor Arneson put the box away.

"I'm sorry," he said.

"Me, too."

As we were leaving the church, I had a thought. "Can we call Mrs. Walker and ask her what happened to the remote?"

Pastor Arneson's face brightened and then clouded over again. "No. She flew up to San Francisco yesterday for her daughter's wedding. She won't be back until Friday morning."

"Can we call her in San Francisco?"

"Caroline mentioned she'd be staying with relatives. I don't know their names and she didn't leave a contact number."

When we walked into the family room at the parsonage, both Linda and her mom looked at us expectantly. They quickly realized we hadn't found what we were looking for. Linda put things into perspective by saying,

"Caroline will be back in a few days, you can ask her when she returns."

The wail of a tiny baby ended all further discussion. We went upstairs to the nursery, where Linda changed her son's diaper and handed him to me. I admired him for several minutes before handing him back to his mother.

"I've taken up enough of your time," I said. "Thank you for your help."

"Mrs. Walker will be in at 9:00 on Friday, I'll ask her about the remote as soon as I see her and either have her give you a call or call you myself,"

Pastor Arneson told me.

"Great," I said, with an enthusiasm I did not feel.

Pastor Arneson walked me to the door.

"By the way. Did you hear Georgia has gone missing?" I asked.

"Sorry, I can't discuss that," he said and his smile faded.

As I walked to my car I realized that if he couldn't comment on Georgia's absence he was probably counseling either her, Veronica or both women. Maybe there was more to that relationship than we knew. I looked at my watch and saw it was only 4:00. I decided to drive up to Santa Barbara and check out beds at the furniture store. I might want to buy something else to put in my condo as well, perhaps a chair or two. Besides the big empty bedroom, I had a big empty living room.

The store seemed to have plenty of beds. I'd forgotten, however, that a bed frame was only the beginning. I'd also need a mattress and box springs, pillows, sheets, blankets and a bedspread. I looked at the prices on sofas and chairs while I was there. By the time I'd added up the minimum amount needed to furnish the condo, I had a severe case of sticker shock. There was no way I could commit myself to spending that much money. Even the cost of just a bed frame, mattress and box springs was more than I wanted to pay.

I fled the store and drove back to Cliffview.

I called Dad as soon as I got home. "How did it go today?"

"The place was a mad house. Lots of calls about the fire and people coming by to inspect the damage or lack thereof. Tons of speculation about why Georgia left, where she is and if she is somehow connected to Cat's murder and the firebombing of our store.

"The police think she left voluntarily. A large suitcase is missing and a window in her bedroom was unlocked. There were no signs of a struggle."

"If Georgia left on her own, why go out a bedroom window?"

"Veronica's bedroom is next to the front door. Opening and closing it might have awakened her.

"Oh, I almost forgot. We got another call about an illegally parked car, a Toyota SUV. I have the license plate number. Did you talk to Linda?"

I told him about the car remote and Mrs. Walker. He was as disappointed as I was that we'd have to wait until Friday, but elated that Linda had remembered what she'd done with the remote. I told him I was having dinner with Danny and Sam and he said he and Sandy were having dinner at her house and going to bed early.

When we disconnected I had just 20 minutes to shower and dress and I did so with great haste. My hair was still wet when the doorbell rang. When I opened it, Danny and Sam stood there, grinning at me. They wore matching dark blue T-shirts with the name of Danny's dive store on them and blue jeans. Danny kissed me on the cheek as he came in.

"Hi Sunshine. Did you sleep?"

"I took a nap."

"We didn't," Sam said. "I helped my dad with his beach class then we went to the shop. Dad had to fix the compressor. How come you don't have any furniture?"

"I looked at some today. I'm just not in any hurry to spend a lot of money."

After I blow dried my hair we drove to the Pizza Parlor in Danny's truck. Danny and I had a couple of beers while I told him about Georgia and my lack of success at finding the remote. We could see Sam in the video arcade.

When the pizza came, we practically inhaled it. In between bites, Sam told me how his dad had rescued one of his students.

"The guy nearly drowned. Dad had to bring him back through the surf. He was huge, too."

By the time we finished the pizza Sam was silent and leaning against his dad. Danny looked at his son and said, "Long day for the kid."

I looked at Danny, "Long day for his dad, too."

"I expect to sleep well tonight," he admitted. The guys dropped me at my condo before continuing on to Sam's mother's house in Ventura. Sam bid me good night as I got out of the truck. Danny walked me to my door and we kissed briefly before he left. Five minutes later, I was in my sleeping bag. Ten minutes later, I was asleep.

Chapter 26

The sound of breaking glass and the smell of gasoline brought me wide awake a few hours later. I knew instantly that a Molotov cocktail had been hurled through my kitchen window.

I rolled out of my sleeping bag and raced for the living room. Flaming gasoline covered the floor, blocking my way to the front door. The fire alarm installed on the ceiling began beeping. I slammed the bedroom door shut and spread my sleeping bag across the bottom to keep the smoke out. I grabbed a pair of jeans and my tennis shoes and went outside on the balcony, closing the sliding glass door behind me. As I hastily pulled on the jeans and slipped my feet into the shoes, I considered my options. My second story balcony was a long way from the ground. Even if I had sheets to tie together, which I didn't, I had nothing to tie them to (namely a bed) that would act as an anchor. Although there was a eucalyptus tree nearby, to reach the sturdiest branch, I'd have to stand on the balcony railing and jump about eight feet. Superwoman I'm not.

Options considered, I quickly decided on a course of action. "Fire!" I screamed. "Help, help, help!"

That awakened a man across the street. He threw up his window and stuck his head out. When I screamed, "Fire, fire!" again, he withdrew his head and vanished from view.

I screamed a few more times. Windows and doors opened. People streamed into the street from condos and homes, gathering on the sidewalk beneath me. Across the street, the man who had seen me from his window hurried out of his backyard in his pajamas, carrying an aluminum ladder. Several people quickly grabbed hold and were soon helping him set it up against my balcony. When I was sure it was secure, I climbed down it.

My feet had no sooner touched the ground than two fire engines roared up, lights flashing and sirens blaring. Several police cars followed. Before long, firemen wearing yellow slickers, helmets and boots climbed onto my balcony from ladders on their trucks. Others entered through the lobby and broke down my door. Armed with water hoses, they quickly put the fire out.

As I stood shivering in the night and watching the spectacle, Dad pushed his way through the crowd to my side. It seemed nearly all of Cliffview had gathered in front of my condo, including Police Chief Lawson and several of his men.

Dad put an arm around me, his face pale and concerned. "Are you all right? I heard the sirens and thought it might be the store again. What happened?"

I was telling him, the fire chief and Lawson what had transpired when the fireman got a call. There was another fire on Seventh Street. Dad and I looked at each other. His face turned ashen.

"Oh no," he said faintly.

Chief Lawson glanced at both of us, then said, "Come with me." We tumbled into his police car. He turned on its lights and its siren and sped off, just ahead of the fire engine. Long before we turned west on Seventh we saw flames lighting the night sky.

The beautiful Victorian house I had grown up in was fully engulfed in fire. The fire crew began spraying water on it shortly after we got there but it was clear the effort was futile. The firemen could only hope to prevent the fire from spreading to other houses.

It is absolutely terrible to watch a big part of your life go up in flames. Dad and I stood side by side with our arms around each other. Dad's face was grim, his jaw clenched. Tears ran down my cheeks.

Chief Lawson walked up and stood beside us.

"We've had three fires, now," I said, my voice shaking with emotion. "Do you still think we're dealing with a teenage prank?"

I saw utter misery on his face in the light of the fire and he seemed to shrink into himself as he watched it.

"Guess you guys better tell me everything you know about the Callahan case. I'll set the entire force to tracing down every lead you have."

"I can't bear to watch this anymore," Dad said. "Let's go to the store."

We got back in Lawson's patrol car and he drove us to Greene's. There, we played the video showing Linda finding the remote (the police had never bothered to watch the copy Dad had given them). Next we gave Lawson the list of the six cars our callers had said were parked illegally the night/early morning before the wedding. Just as we finished, we heard banging on the front door. When we got there, we found Sandy and Danny. Relief flooded their faces when they saw Dad and I were unhurt.

"We've been frantic," Sandy said.

"We went to the condo first, then to the house, looking for you," Danny said. "We didn't know if you were dead or alive."

"One of the firemen at the house told us you'd gone off with Chief Lawson," Sandy continued. "When we went to the police station they said you were here."

"Oh Red, I'm so sorry about the house," Sandy said as she hugged Dad.

"How did you get out of your condo?" Danny asked. He wrapped his arms around me. "One guy said you jumped. But it looked like an awfully long way down. I thought you might be in the hospital."

Somewhere along the line, Chief Lawson slipped away unnoticed.

Eventually, adrenaline gave way to exhaustion. At 3:00 am Danny left, saying that since the dive boat would be leaving the dock in three hours he might as well go on up to Santa Barbara and sleep on it. Dad and I would be staying at Sandy's. I had no desire to spend the night alone, I really needed company.

In Sandy's guest room, I changed into the nightgown she lent me and fell onto the comfortable bed. I slept restlessly; every time I closed my eyes I saw the flickering flames that had destroyed the only real home I'd ever known.

Chapter 27

It was a relief to hear Dad and Sandy moving around about 8:00 am; I had tossed and turned all night and was anxious to get out of bed. I put on a robe I found in the closet and wandered into the kitchen, where freshly made coffee welcomed me. On a counter there were several boxes of cereal so I helped myself to breakfast. A short time later, Sandy and Dad came into the kitchen. They both looked like I felt, half dead. We ate in silence for a while.

Dad was the first to speak. "I'd rather not go into work at all today," he said, running his hands through his hair. "But we have to do it. We'll be inundated with the curious. How do you feel, Cinnamon?"

"Like death warmed over," I admitted. "And short tempered to boot. Do you have something I could wear, Sandy? My clothes smell like smoke and gasoline."

"You can borrow anything I've got," Sandy told me. "I think we're about the same size."

I borrowed a pair of jeans and a striped top from Sandy, along with a pair of socks. A short while later, Sandy dropped me at my condo. She and Dad were going onto the house. I was surprised to find a police car parked outside my building and a policeman sitting on a chair outside the damaged door of my condo.

"The insurance agent is coming by this afternoon. After that the owner can arrange to have your place repaired," the police officer told me. "Looks like you've got mostly water damage."

That was an understatement. The front door was splintered and hanging half off its hinges. The large glass window in the kitchen was shattered. The floors of the living room and kitchen were scorched. Everything was wet. It occurred to me that the unit below mine would have considerable water damage as well.

I walked carefully through the living room and into the bedroom. My sleeping bag was a soggy mess. Like the living room, the floor of the bedroom was dotted with little puddles of water but the clothes in the closet were dry. I'd have to wash them before I wore them, however, because they smelled strongly of smoke. My hard shelled suitcase, on the floor of the closet, was fine once I dried off the outside. I stuffed as much as I could into it. The police officer carried it down to my van in the garage. I thanked him before heading to Greene's. I couldn't bring myself to go past the house.

Dad had gotten to the store just before I did.

"The house is a total loss," he told me. "What's left of the structure is on the brink of collapse." He looked depressed.

"I'm sorry, Dad," I said. "I never realized there might be retaliation when I suggested posting those fliers."

"You couldn't have known something like this would happen, honey. And don't forget, I thought the posters were a good idea, too."

We thought the day after the store was fire bombed was busy but it paled in comparison to the morning after the condo and house burned. It seemed everyone we knew either called or stopped by. We had multiple offers of accommodations and clothing; food arrived by the ton. Around lunchtime, we gave up any hope of doing business. We closed the shop and set up a couple of tables in front of it for the food we'd received. The Starbucks next door offered free coffee while other restaurants in the mall provided free sodas and bottled water. The grocery store gave us paper plates and utensils. Greene's became the center of a huge spontaneous though very somber party.

In late afternoon, everyone pitched in to clean up and the crowd began to disperse.

Afterward, Dad and I drove to Sandy's in my van. A police car was parked across the street. Apparently, Chief Lawson had decided Dad and I were in danger and should be watched.

Dad, Sandy and I flopped on chairs and the sofa and tried to watch TV. They gave up after about an hour. Hoping to hear from Danny, I willed myself to stay awake a while longer. While the *California Diver* should have returned to Santa Barbara about 3:30, he did not call. I left a message on his cell and then, exhausted, went to bed and fell dead asleep. The night passed uneventfully.

Chapter 28

Monday dawned bright and sunny. Danny had called and left a brief and hurried message after I turned off my phone the night before. He said: "I'm going out of town for two or three days. We won't have any cell service so I can't call until I get back. Hope you are doing okay. Miss you."

I wondered who he was going where with and why. I searched my memory for mention of a trip and came up empty. I'd just have to wait until he came home to satisfy my curiosity.

When Dad and I arrived at Greene's we found Chief Lawson sitting in his patrol car in front of the store. He came inside with us.

"Just wanted to update you on the investigation," he said gruffly.

He told us his staff had tracked down the owners of all six cars that had been reported parked illegally on Friday night/early Saturday morning. The one car we had been told was a BMW, however, wasn't. It was, Chief Lawson said, a dark blue Ford. Its owner actually had a permit to park in the restricted area but had just moved in that day and forgotten to put the sticker on his window.

Dad's and my face fell when we heard that. We perked up, however, when we heard that one of the other five cars was a BMW that belonged to Jason Satana.

"Don't get too excited," Chief Lawson warned

us. "Jason's latest girlfriend lives in a condo on Beach Street and he's been spending a lot of time with her. His car has collected tickets for parking without a permit on four consecutive weekends."

He went on to say that official records turned up two more cars that had been ticketed for illegal parking. Neither of them, however, was a BMW.

"We're going to interview all of these people," he told us. "We'll find out why they were parked illegally and if they have any connection to Cat Callahan."

The chief let us digest that information before continuing. "We also found Georgia."

"Where is she?" Dad and I asked in unison.

"In Hawaii. She got married in Vegas last Friday and is on a two-week honeymoon with her new husband. I spoke to her this morning and she sounds ecstatic."

"Married? Who did she marry? I didn't even know she was dating anyone." You could have knocked me over with a feather. A glance at Dad showed he was just as stunned.

"Her new name is Mrs. Andrew Weatherby. She married her postman."

"The guy with the ponytail?" That came from Dad.

"He's an interesting person," Lawson said. "He has PhD in philosophy and once taught at UCSB. He hated being cooped up in a classroom, however, so he became a postman. He loves delivering the mail in Cliffview, where he can be outdoor all day, all year. I've talked to him several times when he was delivering our mail."

"How did he and Georgia get together? I've never heard the slightest whisper that they were dating."

"No one knew about them. A year ago Andy started eating his lunch while reading at book at The Bakery. Veronica suggested he use the employee table behind the shop so he could read without interruption. When the post office changed his lunch hour, he ended up having it at the same time Georgia did. She also ate at the employee table and read. Before long, they put their books down and started talking. Georgia knew that would upset her mother, who managed to discourage every man who ever showed any interest in her only child. When Victoria tried to alienate him, Andy realized what was happening. He concocted a story for Georgia to tell her mother. She was to say he was gay, had once worked as a costume designer on Broadway, and enjoyed discussing art, the theater, books and fashion.

"While Andy is interested in art, the theater and books, he's not gay, nor is he the least bit interested in fashion or designing costumes. But Veronica believed what Georgia told her and not only allowed the friendship to continue she encouraged it.

"The friendship evolved into much more and several nights a week Georgia took to climbing out of her bedroom window to spend time with Andy. He rented an apartment half a block from her house, which made getting together very easy. Georgia knew, though, that they couldn't keep their secret forever and Veronica would become hysterical when she found out. They decided to elope to Las Vegas and take a long honeymoon to allow Veronica to cool off. If that doesn't happen, Georgia and Andy are willing to move to another city or even another state.

"When they arrived on Lanai, Georgia called Pastor Arneson and asked him to tell her mother where she was and why."

"Did Arneson know about Andy?" I asked.

"Not until Georgia called him from Hawaii. That was the best kept secret Cliffview has ever had."

All I could manage after all that was, "Wow. Good for Georgia."

Dad was speechless.

After Lawson left the rest of the morning passed pretty quickly, albeit hazily. I couldn't get over the idea of Georgia married. The manager of my condo called. He said the door and the window were being replaced as we spoke and I should be able to move back in by the weekend.

Dad had an appointment with his insurance agent just before noon.

Just after 1:00, I walked down to The Bakery to get some lunch. I had heard Veronica had hired a new helper and it was once again open. It was wonderful to see Veronica behind the counter, though her smile seemed forced and she appeared dazed. I did not get to meet her new employee, who must have been busy in the kitchen.

I took my deli sandwich back to the store to eat. When I got there, Dad was just returning from his meeting with the insurance agent.

"The good news," he told me, "is that I'm going to get enough money to rebuild. The bad news is there is nothing left. That old wooden house burned just like kindling."

He looked really sad.

"The house doesn't matter," I said. "What matters is that you weren't hurt."

"There is that," he said with a faint smile. "But it's hard to see nearly three decades of your life destroyed."

"I know, Dad. Believe me, I know."

A few minutes later, Dad signaled me to join him and a customer he was talking to. The man was picking up prints he'd had us process.

"This is Dave, Cinnamon. Wait till you see what he's got."

Dave had color photos of parked cars. He'd taken three photos of each one. A side view clearly showed each car in front of his apartment building and a "Parking by permit only" sign. There were also front and back views of each car, showing the license plates.

Dave was eager to tell his story. "My wife and I have one parking space and two cars. I've got a permit that allows me to park on the street. We live only a couple of blocks from the church where Cat died.

"I work the graveyard shift at Santa Barbara General's emergency room. Many times when I get home, especially on the weekend mornings, there is no place for my car near my building because there are so many illegally parked cars. Lots of people have friends spending the night.

"I tried calling the police. Only they don't get there early enough to ticket the cars. So, the last couple of weeks I've been taking photos. The prints have the date and time on them. I'm going to show them to the police.

"I saw one of your fliers a couple of days ago and thought you might want to see the prints, too. Check these out. They show the three cars parked illegally in my area on the morning of the wedding." He spread nine photos on the counter. One was a black BMW, probably Jason's.

"That one's been there four weekends in a row," Dave told us.

One of the other cars was a dark blue Ford; the third one was a slate blue BMW.

"That's Megan Mauvais' car," I said, pointing to the BMW.

Dad whistled. "Are you sure?"

"Very sure. I went down to check out its license plates Friday morning, remember? It has personalized plates that stand for Megan's Hair and Nails."

Before Dave went on to the police station, we got his permission to print another set of photos just for us.

After he left, I looked at Dad. "Now all we have to do is find that remote."

On the off chance that Pastor Arneson's secretary had returned early, I phoned him. While he hadn't heard from Mrs. Walker, he volunteered to see if she was home. He called us back in five minutes. He said no one had answered the phone and he'd left a message asking Caroline to call him as soon as she got in.

Dad, Sandy and I decided to go to the Italian place in town for dinner that night. When they suggested I invite Danny I told them about his mystery trip.

On our return to Sandy's house, we found a Cliffview police car parked across the street. The officer waved to us and we waved back. We were grateful for his presence.

The three of us spent a quiet, uneventful evening watching TV. I turned in just before midnight. About 3:00 am I awoke from a restless sleep with tears rolling down my cheeks. While I couldn't remember the dream that caused them I had trouble drifting back to sleep.

Chapter 29

Tuesday morning, the three of us discussed the Wednesday Warriors trip over cinnamon raisin bagels and coffee. I didn't want to go without Danny. Dad and Sandy decided not to go either. Dad wanted to go through what was left of the house before it was torn down.

"I keep hoping I'll find something," he said. "I can't believe everything's gone."

After breakfast, we took my van to the store. Just before noon, as I was helping a customer decide which compact point and shoot camera to buy, Mike Takamura came over and whispered in my ear, "Your husband would like to have a word with you."

That was a shocking statement. My head jerked up involuntarily and I saw Ted standing by one of the counters. He lifted a hand and produced a half-hearted wave. He looked glum. What on Earth did he want?

The man I was helping had trouble making up his mind, so it was a good 15 minutes before I was free. Ted waited patiently, in itself a sign that all was not well with him. He hated waiting and didn't usually do it gracefully.

Finally, I was free. "Ted. What are you doing here?"

"Good to see you, too, Cinnamon," he said, putting an arm around me and planting a kiss on my cheek. It had been intended for my mouth but I managed to turn my head at the last minute. "God I've missed you. Can we go somewhere? We need to talk."

I suggested lunch at Juanita's. We walked the short distance to the restaurant.

Along the way Ted asked, "How are you doing, Cinnamon? You look tired." He seemed sincere. I was almost taken in by that before I remembered he had the sympathy act down pat. He'd perfected it on me.

I hadn't planned on telling him what had happened, it just came tumbling out.

Ted stopped dead in his tracks and stared at me. "Someone is trying to kill you and Red? Maybe you should start at the beginning, Cinnamon."

We had reached Juanita's by now and the hostess showed us to a booth. I scooted over to the window on one side of the table, expecting Ted to sit on the other. Instead, he slid in next to me and took my right hand in both of his.

"Now what's this about a dead bride, fliers and fires?"

I began telling him. A waitress brought us ice water and came back a few minutes later to take our orders. Without much thought, we both ordered the special and I continued my story.

Ted was mesmerized. Our lunches arrived and grew cold. Near the end, when I got to the part about the condo and the house burning, I broke down and began to cry. Ted put his arm around me and held me until I calmed down.

"My God," he said. "You've been through hell.

Makes my problems look like squat. I'd take you home with me if I had a home to take you to."

"What happened to the Hollywood house?" I asked, blowing my nose on a tissue from my purse.

"My new manager didn't pay the rent and the landlord kicked us out."

"What about the studio?" I asked.

Ted didn't meet my eyes. "Ditto," he said, moving his silverware around aimlessly on his placemat.

"How's Willow?"

"She left when we were evicted." His eyes remained downcast.

"Still have your little sport car?"

"The girls, uh, forgot to make the payments on it, too."

"So the dealer took it back," I said. Ted nodded. He looked even more miserable than I felt.

"You took care of everything, Cinnamon. You paid the rent, you made the car payments, you billed the clients. I didn't realize there were so many things to take care of or that it would be so hard for someone else to do."

"No one billed the clients?"

"Very little money has come in since you left."

I sat in stunned silence, absorbing what he'd said.

"You kept my life on track, Cinnamon. You were always there for me. I didn't appreciate you until you left. Believe me, I've really missed you."

"Do you miss me or just the services I provided?"

Ted met my eyes and the pain on his face looked real. "I miss *you* and all you did.

159

"I'm staying with one of our Windgate classmates," he continued. "Remember Steve McFarland?"

I nodded.

"Well, someone recorded that Tonight Show appearance and sent me a copy of it. I thought it would be cool to show it to Steve. I remembered that night as being a lot of fun. But my God, I was an asshole. No wonder you left."

"So what happens now?" I asked. I was shocked by how far Ted had fallen in so short a time.

The intensity in Ted's eyes was surprising. "I came here to beg you to give me another chance, Cinnamon. I want us to be together again. I swear, it will be different this time. I'll walk the straight and narrow. I also came to beg for your help. You're the only one who can get me out of this mess."

"I've already given you a zillion chances, Ted. You always make the same promises. You never come close to keeping them."

"I know I'm lower than the lowest form of life on Earth. I don't have any right to ask you for anything. I shouldn't have come." He started to get up.

In the years I'd known Ted I had never seen him genuinely humble before. It took me aback. I reached for his hand and he sat back down. I was silent for a few minutes, struggling with the warring sides of my mind. One said let him sink, he deserves it; the other said help him one last time, it's the right thing to do. The better side won.

"I'll help you get your business back on track," I said at last. "We are, however, still getting divorced. I don't love you anymore. I've found someone else."

Ted's expression shifted from elation to dejection. "I guess I'll have to take whatever you're willing to give. You sure don't owe me anything."

Our lunches were cold when we began to eat them. Neither of us talked until we finished.

"I'll give you a crash course on how to run your business," I told him. "Starting with the billing. I'll show you how it's done but you have to collect the money. When you have enough, you can rent another studio and try to win back your clients. I will hire at least one person to help you. Someone with actual qualifications for the job.

"If you'd done your own homework in college instead of asking me to do it, you'd already know how to run your business."

The little black cloud that had formed over Ted's head seemed to dissipate. "Will you come back to LA with me today?"

"I'll come down tomorrow, it's my day off. If Jeannie will have me, I'll stay with her. I'll work with you only as long as I think necessary," I warned him. "After that, it's up to you. And if there's any screwing around, I'm gone and I'm never, ever coming back."

Ted opened his mouth to say something and decided against it. He gave me Steve's address and phone number; I told him I'd call him when I got to Jeannie's.

Ted stood up and slid out of the booth. Then he looked at me sheepishly. "Can I borrow some money? I'm driving Steve's car and it's almost out of gas."

I gave him a couple of $20s. He kissed me on the cheek, whispered, "You're wonderful" in my ear then left with a spring in his step. I paid the lunch check and went back to Greene's.

The rest of the day went slowly. I told Dad my plans and, as I expected, he advised against them. I called Jeannie and she said I could stay at her house as long as I wanted. She was not thrilled to hear I'd be helping Ted, however.

"He sure knows how to get to you, Cinnamon," she said. "A few days with him and you'll be right back where you started."

"Not a chance, Jeannie. I'll tell you why when I get there."

The reason, of course, was Danny.

Chapter 30

As I drove down to the big city I played my country tapes, singing along with them and refusing to think about Danny. Not that I knew anything more about his disappearance.

I stopped at Jeannie's first, staying only long enough to drop off my overnight bag and kiss the baby. I told her not to wait up for me. Then I drove to Hollywood.

One of Ted's roommates was a car magazine editor/photographer; the other was an editor for a hunting magazine published by the same company.

The men rented an old two-bedroom California cottage. The yard and house looked neglected. The grass was brown and there were no shrubs or flowers, just a couple of unhappy looking palm trees. The house needed paint and major repairs.

Ted answered the door. He seemed very happy and relieved to see me and I realized he'd been afraid I'd change my mind about helping him. I noticed now that he was quite a bit thinner than he'd been the last time I saw him at the Hollywood Hills house.

The inside of his latest abode had a cluttered, bachelor-pad look. The furniture was thrift store vintage and empty beer bottles and partially filled coffee cups were everywhere. Ted was sleeping on a well-worn sofa and his photo equipment took up most of the garage.

A few days earlier, I'd heard a Windgate

professor telling Greene's Mike Takamura about a man who had made a pile of money at age 29 by selling a dot-com he'd started. He'd just graduated Windgate and was embarking on what he hoped was a less stressful career in portrait photography. He'd bought a building in Hollywood and set up his new business. All he needed now were clients.

I thought the dot-com entrepreneur might be interested in working with an established photographer (Ted) while building his portfolio. He would learn a lot from Ted and Ted would benefit from the other man's business skills.

Mike knew the new graduate's name, Brad Bronwell, because he'd been a Greene's customer when he was a student. I interviewed Bronwell over the phone and he had agreed to have dinner with Ted and me tonight. I'd also asked Ted to find certain files and set up the studio computer. It now sat on the coffee table with the files piled beside it.

I'd expected the files to be a mess. They were, however, pretty much the way I'd left them. The women Ted had hired to take over for me had apparently done little to nothing with them. I showed Ted where everything was and explained what he needed to do. I wasn't sure he understood everything I'd said, but if I found the right person to help him, that wouldn't matter too much. When I finished, it was time for dinner.

We met Brad at a nearby Denny's. There was no point in going anywhere nicer, Brad needed to know what he was getting into from the start. Short, stocky and balding, Brad was excited and enthusiastic about his new venture. He was in awe of Ted, whose legend lived on at Windgate despite his recent hard times. I thought they'd make a good team. The skills one lacked, the other had.

The two men seemed to get on quite well. We continued the meeting, with more privacy, at Brad's pricey apartment on the Sunset Strip. You could see our old house from it. There, I provided an assessment of Ted's good points and his failings. While Ted squirmed a lot he admitted my assessment was accurate. Brad was optimistic he could deal with an imperfect genius who slept with his female clients, was rarely on time for anything, had no money sense whatsoever, and no interest in doing anything other than "making beautiful images" and enjoying a celebrity lifestyle. A couple of hours later, the two men agreed to go into business together. Brad's lawyer would craft an agreement both would sign that would help keep Ted on the straight and narrow, something I had never been able to do.

Before we left, Brad told us he'd be over first thing in the morning with a rental truck so we could move all of Ted's equipment to his studio.

Ted walked me to my van and we spent several minutes standing next to it and talking. He had dropped the phony Hollywood mannerisms and vocabulary he'd adopted a couple years earlier and seemed much more like the old Ted; the talented student photographer I'd fallen in love with.

As I was getting into my van he said, "It's been really good seeing you, Cinnamon. I've missed you more than you can know."

I opened my mouth to say something but he held up a hand to stop me.

"I know what you're thinking. Yes, I missed you taking care of business, that's obvious. I hope I've made it clear I've also missed you. I know I've been a total asshole. I don't deserve another chance but can't we give it one more try?"

He took my face in his hands and kissed me. It was a sincere, intense, heartfelt kiss and made me feel....nothing, absolutely nothing. It wasn't like kissing Danny. Now that was something.

When he finished, Ted searched my face.

"I'm sorry, Ted. You're several years too late."

He picked up my hand and kissed it. "See you tomorrow."

He watched me drive off. While it was too dark to see his face, the slump of his shoulders telegraphed how he felt.

On the way to Jeannie's I started crying, thinking about what might have been.

All was quiet at Jeannie and Dave's house. Dave had already gone to work when I awoke the next morning. While Jeannie already had a pretty good idea of what had happened in Cliffview she wanted a first hand account. She found mine astounding.

"I thought you were going back to a nice safe place, Cinnamon. Instead there's been chaos. A bride killed? Fires started by a murderer? Please, please be careful. I'll worry about you until the murderer/arsonist is caught."

After breakfast, Jeannie cleaned up while I gave Alexa her bath. When I'd left two months earlier it seemed impossible that the baby could get any cuter and yet she had. She was absolutely adorable and Jeannie and I were sure she recognized me. During her nap, I told her mother about Danny. She was excited and happy for me, right up until the time I told her he'd left town on a mystery trip and I hadn't talked to him for several days. When I finished, I waited for her input. Jeannie said she needed time to process what I'd told her and she'd let me know her thoughts the next day. I had a bad feeling about that.

Chapter 31

Dave, Jeannie and Alexa were up early. They tried to be quiet but it's a little house. I wandered out into the kitchen after Dave left. Alexa was in her playpen and Jeannie was loading the dishwasher. She set a glass of orange juice, a cup of coffee and an English muffin in front of me. She knew it was futile to attempt conversation before I'd had a dose of caffeine.

I drank the juice, toasted, buttered and ate the muffin, then downed the coffee. Feeling better, I said, "Thanks, Jeannie. You truly are a wonderful friend."

"Good morning to you, too. When do you have to be at Ted's?"

"Brad will call when he heads for the Ted's house. Have you had time to think about Danny and me?"

She had. "You know what your biggest problem is, Cinnamon?"

"No, though I get the impression you're about to tell me."

"You're damn right. You always let Ted walk all over you. If you'd thrown a fit the first time he fooled around it probably would have been the last." Jeannie had been winding up, now she delivered her pitch. She stood there in her kitchen, an indignant look on her face and her hands on her hips.

"Your new boyfriend has pulled the disappearing act. It sounds like Ted all over again."

"Danny isn't like Ted at all."

"So you say. You're falling for this guy aren't you?"

"Yes. Most definitely. Probably already fallen."

"Then save yourself from future difficulties by not putting up with any shit now."

While Jeannie had probably planned a longer lecture, my phone rang. It was Ted, telling me Brad was on his way over.

"I'll be there in a few minutes," I told him. "Gotta go," I told Jeannie, getting up and walking toward my bedroom.

"You think about what I said, Cinnamon Greene," Jeannie called after me. "You know I'm right."

A few minutes later, I was out the door. And I did think about what she'd said as I drove to Ted's.

The men had already begun loading the truck when I got there. The more I got to know Brad, the better I liked him. He was a down to earth, no nonsense kind of person who was probably an excellent photo technician and obviously had good business sense. Ted would be the creative force in their partnership and Brad would be the money man.

We worked steadily, stopping only for a quick lunch at McDonald's. Somewhere around 7:00 pm, everything had been unloaded at the new studio. The men could figure out where to put it the next day.

Brad and Ted wanted to celebrate their new partnership by going out to dinner, which Brad offered to pay for. I, however, was anxious to get back to Cliffview. I had a small sip of the champagne Brad produced and told the guys I was going home. I let Brad know he could call me with questions any time though I doubted I'd hear from him. We'd both learned the business side of photography from the same place and I was sure he'd do well.

Ted walked me to my van. I got in and rolled down the window. Ted thanked me again and kissed me on the cheek. He stood on the curb as I drove off, looking sad. I hoped it was genuine.

The sun had set over the ocean by the time I got to the Pacific Coast Highway. There was little traffic and I made good time. My vintage country music pals, the Judds, helped. It's always good to know you're not alone when it comes to dealing with men, that other women have trouble doing it successfully, too. I knew Jeannie was right. The problem was that I've always been considerably braver in thought than actual deed.

Dad and Sandy had just gotten back from their health club when I arrived at her house. A police car was stationed across the street and I waved to the cop who sat inside.

I told Dad and Sandy about Ted's new partner. Then I asked if there'd been any messages.

"The manager of your condo building called. He said you should be able to move back into your apartment sometime next week."

"That's great," I said. "And I'm going to see Mrs. Walker about the remote first thing tomorrow."

There was a moment of silence then Sandy said, "Red and I have something to tell you, Cinnamon." She looked at Dad.

He blushed before blurting out, "Sandy and I are getting married. We're going to build a new house on the old lot."

"That's wonderful," I said. And to my surprise, I really meant it. "Have you set a date?"

"It will be some time in February," Sandy said. "We're going skiing in Sun Valley for our honeymoon. We'd love to have you and a friend come along. Red says you're a good skier. We'll have fun."

"I haven't skied in years. I'll have to think about that." I hesitated a minute. "Did Danny call?"

"No," Dad and Sandy said in unison.

"He's back in town," Sandy said. "I saw him in the grocery store this afternoon. He was in a hurry. I mentioned you'd be back tonight."

"What did he say?" I asked.

"He didn't say anything."

"Did he say where he'd been?"

"No," Sandy said. "It was a very brief encounter."

We all settled down in front of the TV. At least Dad and Sandy settled down. I felt restless. Suddenly, I couldn't wait any longer, I had to see Danny. Otherwise I'd never get any sleep.

"I've got to go out," I said.

"Where?" Dad asked, surprised.

"Don't worry about me, okay?"

As I left the room I heard Sandy say, "She's going to see Danny, Red."

I drove over to Cliffview Divers. Danny's truck was there and through the store's open back door, I could see him moving about. It looked like he was alone. I parked and went inside.

Danny looked up when I came in but didn't stop

putting things away and didn't look at me again.

I didn't know where to begin. Finally I said, "Danny, can we talk?"

"I don't know what there is to talk about," he said stiffly, hanging up a wetsuit.

"Well for starters, you can tell me where you've been and with whom. I'd also like to know why you didn't call me when you got home."

Now Danny looked at me, an angry expression on his face. "Why didn't you tell me you were still married?"

"I thought I did. If I didn't, I'm sorry, it was an oversight. I thought everyone knew. The divorce papers were filed before I moved here and the divorce will be final in four months."

"I walked by Juanita's last Tuesday, Cinnamon. "I saw a guy with his arms around you. Didn't look like someone you were divorcing to me."

"I was telling Ted about the fires and I just kind of lost it," I explained. "I hadn't slept well the night before."

I hesitated before continuing. "Ted and I are friends. I expect we always will be. I've known him a long time. He came up here to ask me to help him get his business up and running again. It fell apart after I left."

"And of course you said 'yes' to your husband," Danny said sarcastically.

"Ted was pretty pathetic. He had no car, no studio and no money. He was sleeping on a friend's couch. I went to LA to help him get back on his feet."

"You're not moving back there?"

"Of course not. The thought never crossed my

mind."

"Oh," Danny had finished stowing gear. He put his hands in his pockets and looked at me, managing a weak smile.

"Now, why don't you tell me why you left town," I said. "Where did you go? Who did you go with?"

Danny sighed and looked at the floor. "My ex-wife called as the *California Diver* was docking last week. She gave me some news that threw me for a loop. Her fiancé has been looking for work for several months and finally found a job in San Francisco. He's moving there in a few days. Sam and his mom will join him next month. Sam knows we won't see each other as often as we do now. He took the news very hard. I did, too. Neither of us wants to be so far apart."

"Can you get full custody?"

"If she was a bad mother, I would. But she does a great job. And Sam loves both of us."

"Where did you go?"

"I took Sam to a friend's cabin near Ojai. We went hiking and horseback riding. I think I managed to convince him everything will be okay, now I just have to convince myself."

"When did you get back?"

"Tuesday morning. I came by Greene's and Mike said you'd just left for Juanita's. He didn't tell me you had company so I walked down there."

"And you saw me with Ted," I finished.

"Right," Danny said. "Later I heard you'd gone to LA with him. People say he's a famous celebrity photographer. I couldn't think of a reason you'd come back here."

"I can tell you one," I said.

I walked over to Danny and put my arms around his waist. He put his arms around me tentatively. "Ted kissed me when I was in LA," I said, "And I'm glad he did."

Danny stiffened. "Why?"

"Because I realized I like kissing you a whole lot more."

Relief flooded his face and he grinned that wicked grin of his. Then he kissed me.

"How was that?" he asked after awhile. "Better than Ted?"

"Ted who? What are you doing tonight? Could you use company?"

"I might be able to find time in my busy schedule for you," Danny said.

Chapter 32

Cheerful whistling emanating from the kitchen awoke me. Well, no one's perfect. That coffee probably awaited me was a serious incentive to get out of bed. I washed my face and combed my hair, then wandered out into the kitchen and sat down at the table.

"Good morning Sunshine," Danny said. He poured a cup of coffee and set it in front of me.

"Don't talk, just nod. Would you like some orange juice?" I nodded. He opened the fridge, removed a carton of juice and poured some in a glass. Next he asked, "Cereal or English muffin?"

"Cereal." In a few minutes, cereal and milk were set before me. Danny sat down at the table and picked up the sports section of the Santa Barbara News-Press. He read it as he sipped coffee. I drank my orange juice, ate my cereal and drained my coffee cup. I got up and refilled my cup, pouring some fresh brew in Danny's cup as well.

When I sat back down I said, "Today's the day."

"For what?"

"We find out what Arneson's secretary did with the BMW remote Linda gave her. I want to be at the church when she comes in. What time is it?"

Danny looked at his watch. "Just after 8:00."

"I better get going," I said. "I need to change clothes at Sandy's first. I'm moving back into my condo next week. Oh. Did I tell you Dad and Sandy are getting married? Do you ski?"

Danny looked up at me, trying to process all the information he'd just heard. "Do I ski?"

I went over and sat in his lap. "Just answer the question."

"Yes, I do ski. Or rather, I did. I haven't gone in years. Why?"

I gave him a kiss, which lasted considerably longer than I'd expected. When it ended I looked at Danny's watch. "I've got to go," I said. I untangled myself and headed off to the bedroom.

As I walked out the door a few minutes later Danny said, "Why did you want to know if I skied?"

"We've been invited to go on Dad and Sandy's honeymoon. They're going skiing in Sun Valley."

I was at the church well before the appointed time. I parked and went to Arneson's office. The church secretary was quite punctual, arriving at exactly 9:00. When we heard her come in, Arneson and I got up and went into her office.

Caroline Walker was a well-padded, petite woman in her early 60s with short, silver hair. She smiled pleasantly when Pastor Arneson introduced us.

"Nice to meet you," she said to me. To Arneson she said, "I got your message to call when I got home last night, Pastor. But my flight was late and I didn't want to wake you."

"We need to ask you about a remote Linda gave you on the day of Cat's wedding," Arneson said.

Mrs. Walker looked at him blankly. "Come again?"

Pastor Arneson added some background. "On the day Cat Callahan got married, Linda found a BMW keyless remote. She says she gave it to you and asked you to put it in the lost and found."

"So much happened that day," Mrs. Walker said slowly. "Cat got married and died and Linda had the baby. There were so many people. I'm afraid I don't remember any remote. Did you look in the lost and found?"

"It's not there," I said. "Where else might it be?"

"I might have put it in my purse, intending to put it in the lost and found later."

"Can you look?" I asked impatiently, indicating the big brown leather purse that sat on her desk.

"That's not the one I had at the wedding." Mrs. Walker frowned. "I wore my green suit and my black pumps so I would have carried one of my black purses."

"And where would they be?" Arneson asked.

"Why at home, of course," Mrs. Walker said a bit indignantly.

"The remote could be really important, Caroline," Pastor Arneson explained. "It might be a clue that could help solve Cat's murder. We're a bit impatient because we've waited several days for you to come back from your trip so we could ask you about it."

Mrs. Walker's ruffled feathers relaxed a bit. "Should I go look for it now?"

"If it's okay with Pastor for you to take some time off, I can drive you there," I said.

Arneson didn't object. The drive took about 10 minutes. Mrs. Walker's mobile home park, designed for senior citizens, was east of the Pacific Coast Highway, on the opposite side of town from the church and just five minutes from Danny's house.

I parked my van in the driveway of Mrs. Walker's double wide and she led me inside. Framed photos of family members and pets were everywhere. I browsed the gallery as she disappeared into her bedroom. She returned with two black purses.

"I can't remember which of these I used," she said, holding a medium sized leather purse in her left hand and a smaller black velvet purse in her right.

"Why don't you just dump them out on the coffee table one at a time? If you see the remote, don't touch it, we should do this the way the cops would."

I took a pair of yellow rubber gloves out of my purse and pulled them on. While I know the police use the surgical versions to handle evidence, these were the only ones I could find in the grocery store.

"If we see the remote, let me pick it up. I even brought a bag to put the evidence in." I produced a small, unused brown paper lunch bag.

"I probably carried this one," Mrs. Walker said. She picked up the largest purse, opened it and upended it on the table. We sorted through what came out of it. There was a comb, a lipstick, some tissues and a pack of gum, but no remote. The pockets and compartments yielded nothing more.

Mrs. Walker put everything back in the first purse and emptied the second one on the table. No keyless remote appeared in its contents, either. I searched the two inside compartments. The only thing I found was a dime.

"Damn," I said, dropping the purse on the table. It landed with a muted clunk.

"What was that?" I asked.

I picked up the purse and shook it. There was something inside.

"That purse has a hole in the lining. Sometimes things get stuck in it," Mrs. Walker exclaimed.

"It's in there," I yelped. "I can feel it. But I can't get it out." I was ready to rip the bag apart when Mrs. Walker grabbed it.

"I know where the opening is," she said, giving me a reproachful look.

"Wait," I warned. "Put on a glove first."

I took off one of mine and handed it to her. She pulled on the glove before putting her hand in the purse. After a couple of seconds she drew her hand out. Her gloved fingers held a quarter. She put it on the table and put her hand back inside the purse. When she pulled it out again, her fingers held a car's keyless remote.

It had a BMW logo on it and looked like the one I remembered.

"Bingo," I said, trying not to jump up and down.

Mrs. Walker looked smug. "I never lose anything," she said. "But I can't always find everything right away."

I opened the lunch bag and held it out so Mrs. Walker could drop her prize in it.

"You did great," I said enthusiastically, giving her a hug. Then I gave her an abbreviated account of all that had happened while she was in San Francisco.

"No wonder you wanted to find that remote so badly," she commented when I finished. "One murder and three fire bombings. It's got to be Jason, don't you think? I've never liked that man."

"He is my prime suspect."

We got back in my van and drove toward the main part of town. I intended to take the remote to the police station and hand it to Chief Lawson. Caroline could verify my account of where it was found. As we neared the mall, however, another idea struck me.

"Megan's car is usually parked right behind her shop," I told Mrs. Walker.

"Let's go try the remote," she suggested.

I drove to the back of the mall. As it had been when I was checking its license plates, Megan's car was behind her shop. I parked at the curb and got out of the van. Before I could tell her to stay put, Mrs. Walker got out, too. I put a glove on my right hand. Unfortunately, it was the glove for the left hand. I didn't bother to change it. I took the remote out of the bag. Then, having no idea how far away a keyless remote could be and still work, I walked toward the vehicle. When I got within ten feet, I pressed a button. There was a loud click.

Mrs. Walker grabbed my hand and pointed to another button. "Try this one."

I pushed the one she indicated and the trunk popped open. We looked at each other in amazement and gave each other high fives.

"I think we've got it." I was filled with elation.

Giddy with success, I threw caution to the wind. I walked up to the car, opened the driver's side door and got in, using the remote to start the engine. I raised my fist in victory and Mrs. Walker gave me a return salute. I had turned the engine off and was halfway out of the car when the door to the salon opened. Megan stood there. Mrs. Walker and I froze.

Megan's face twisted into something that was not at all pretty.

"You," she hissed, walking toward me. "What are you doing? Get away from my car."

I started to back off but Megan lunged at me.

"Haven't you caused enough trouble?" she screamed. "Why do you keep sticking your nose in other people's business?"

She grabbed my left arm and I suddenly realized what lethal weapons those acrylic nails can be. Megan saw the remote about the same time I remembered I held it. I tossed it underhand to Mrs. Walker. "Get in the van and lock the doors," I yelled.

She proved surprisingly agile, first catching the remote in an amazing move and then sprinting toward the van while I tussled with the beautician. Although she was slender, Megan was quite strong.

Attracted by the noise, women came out of the salon. Some of them had curlers in their hair. All wore the salon's pink cover-ups. The women stood and stared as Megan flailed at me, raking a handful of fingernails down the side of my face and drawing blood. I backed away, holding my gloved hand in front of my face. Megan scratched at me and snarled.

I'd never been in a fight in my life but I knew I was losing this one. I did the only thing I could think of, I kicked Megan, first with one foot and then the other. I regretted wearing jogging shoes, which muted the impact. It did slow her down a bit, however, and kept her from seeing Mrs. Walker sneak up behind her carrying the umbrella she had found in my van. It wasn't one of those flimsy lightweight models but a sturdy golf umbrella with a hardwood J-handle.

Megan was inching toward me when Mrs. Walker whacked her on the head with the handle.

Megan let out a scream of outrage and turned to see who her new assailant was. Mrs. Walker hit her again and I kicked her as hard as I could in the back. She turned toward me, grabbing my gloved hand. The glove came off and both of us went down. My fall was broken by Mrs. Walker, who had somehow gotten behind me. The two of us landed in a heap on the ground. Luckily, Mrs. Walker has a low center of gravity and it's well padded. Megan, however, hit her head on the asphalt. She didn't move right away.

"Call the police," I yelled.

"We're already here," Chief Lawson said. He sounded disgusted. "What the hell is going on?"

Mrs. Walker and I untangled our limbs. I stood up and Lawson helped Caroline regain her footing.

"Are you okay?" I asked.

"I'm fine," she said, brushing off her pants. "We found the keyless remote, Chief, and it works on her car." She pointed to Megan, who was sitting up slowly.

To me she confided, "I got the idea about hitting her with the umbrella from the Amelia Peabody mysteries."

"Ah," I said. "The parasol wielding lady Egyptologist. I love those books, too."

Meanwhile, there was a puzzled look on Lawson's face.

"You found the remote? When? Where was it?"

"It's a long story," I said.

After checking to make sure a now glowering Megan didn't need emergency room treatment,

Lawson shooed all the beauty salon's customers and employees back inside the shop and invited Megan, Mrs. Walker and me to come down to the police station. Actually, it was less an invitation than a command.

Before we left, I suggested the chief see for himself that the remote worked. Wearing one of my yellow rubber gloves, he carried it over to Megan's car.

When the car started, Mrs. Walker and I hugged each other and jumped up and down like little kids.

A few minutes later, we were on our way to the police station. There, the remote was logged in as evidence and sent to the lab. Mrs. Walker and I gave our statements separately and had our fingerprints taken.

"So many people have handled it that it's highly unlikely we'll find any usable prints. But if we do, we'll need to know which are yours," Lawson told us.

He also said that the previous day he and his officers had interviewed all of the people whose cars had been parked illegally the night before the wedding. As expected, Jason claimed he had been staying with his girlfriend. She backed him up, saying he was with her all night and they didn't part until after breakfast the next morning.

Except for Megan, all the other illegal parkers had similar alibis. She first said she had not parked her car in that neighborhood on the night in question. When confronted with a dated photo and two calls logged to the police complaining about it being parked illegally, Megan claimed the car must have been taken without her knowledge and mysteriously returned to its parking space behind her salon. She couldn't explain how that could have been done.

"We don't believe any of that," Lawson said. "Megan is being interviewed again right now. It will be interesting to hear how she explains her remote being found on church property when she didn't attend the wedding."

"Before we go, I'd appreciate knowing why you suspected Veronica and Georgia," I said.

Lawson hesitated. He worded his reply carefully, giving us the gist of what happened but not the details.

"Two days after Cat's murder, a member of the mayor's extended family came to see me. She said that while the mayor was vehemently opposed to her visit, there were things she thought I should know.

"It seems there had been a major falling out between Victoria and Georgia over financial assets. They had already been to counseling with limited success. In desperation, Georgia appealed to the mayor, Margo and Cat for help. All four confronted Victoria and convinced her to give Georgia the autonomy she requested. Victoria, however, deeply resented her brother and sister-in-law's meddling. She was so angry the family member feared she might have punished them by killing their only child.

"We knew from her first interview that Georgia was hiding something. She is normally a straightforward person, yet she was she was agonizingly reluctant to tell us anything. We thought that meant she knew Victoria had killed Cat.

"We were wrong about that," Lawson admitted. "It wasn't until she eloped with the mailman that we realized Georgia's secret had nothing to do with Cat's murder."

I said: "I'm amazed there was any turmoil in Veronica and Georgia's lives. They were always pleasant to customers and each other and appeared happy."

"Things are not always what they seem," Lawson intoned.

Caroline and I walked to Greene's from the police station and I drove her to the church, where we parted with a hug. I went back Greene's, where everyone already knew about the remote and my fight with Megan. They winced at the scratches on my face and seemed surprised I wasn't in a full body cast. The accounts they heard, it seemed, had been somewhat exaggerated.

Later, Dad said, "Danny's phoned several times. He's anxious to talk to you."

"I heard all sorts of wild stories," Danny said when I called him. "I was afraid you'd be in a wheelchair for life."

"Why don't we have dinner together? That way you can see for yourself that I'm nearly perfect, or as near perfect as I'll ever be."

"Are you buying?"

"Maybe."

In late afternoon, Lawson called. "Thought you'd like to know that we searched Megan's house a couple of hours ago. At all three fires the incendiary device was a bottle of a particular brand and type of wine that had been filled with gasoline. Megan orders that wine by the case and we found several bottles of it.

"We also found a pair of black sweatpants and a black sweatshirt on her balcony. They smelled of gasoline. We're pretty sure she wore those clothes the nights she started the fires."

"Did she confess to anything?"

"No. She lawyered up not long after you left. But we've got enough evidence to charge her with the fire bombings and will probably have enough soon to charge her with Cat's murder as well."

During dinner at Juanita's I told Danny about Georgia, Veronica and Andy and described the day's adventures, interrupted only a couple of times by townsfolk mostly interested in my battle scars. They consisted of three superficial scratches on my face, several scratches on my arms and a rather large bruise on my left hip, which no one except Danny will ever see.

"You took quite a chance trying that remote on Megan's car," Danny said when I finished. "She'd killed one person and fire bombed three buildings. You're just about fearless, aren't you?"

"Maybe just not very bright," I admitted. "Besides, Mrs. Walker was there to defend me."

Danny laughed. "While I've never met her, I already love her."

He changed the subject. "What are you doing tonight?"

"Nothing."

"Come to Flanagan's with me. It's country music night. There will be line dancing and barbecued tri-tip."

If I had any doubts Danny and I might have a future together, that conversation did a lot to ease them. A man who's got a good sense of humor, can catch and cook lobsters, and likes dancing to country music is just about perfect.

Acknowledgments

Writing is a solitary exercise. Those who write fiction spend a great deal of time alone with the characters they create. It is all too easy to retreat into that imaginary world and forget that interaction with the living is absolutely necessary for one's mental and physical health.

I am grateful for the support of family and friends. None of them expressed the slightest doubt I would eventually publish a work of fiction, even though I wasn't sure that would ever come to pass.

Thanks to everyone who read this book before it was published, offering corrections, comments and suggestions. I am deeply indebted to all of you, most especially Pamela Cardone, Michael Cardone, Judy Hemenway, Rosemary Kurtti, Verna Suit and Linda Whipple. Any mistakes are mine and mine alone.

About the Author

Bonnie J. Cardone grew up in Arizona, Chicago and Michigan. Six years after she moved to Southern California, she became a scuba diver. From then on, her goal was to dive as much of the world as possible.

After being a stay at home mom for 11 years, Bonnie joined the editorial staff of Skin Diver, the world's largest and oldest diving magazine. (Alas, it is no more.) The 22 years she worked there were exciting and educational. The magazine and the sport grew far larger far faster than anyone expected. Bonnie wrote hundreds of articles on almost every imaginable marine related subject. After she became proficient at topside and underwater photography, most of the articles were illustrated with her images.

When Bonnie was downsized in 1999, she did what she had always planned to do: she started writing mystery novels. She had already taken five UCLA Extension writing classes and written several short mystery stories. At friend Gary Brandner's suggestion, she had become a member of Mystery Writers of America in 1973. She joined Sisters in Crime in 1999 and, in 2000, became the editor of its national newsletter, a job that lasted nine years and provided a first class education in all aspects of the mystery field. During that time Bonnie attended two to three mystery conventions every year, meeting and photographing well-known mystery writers. She also attended author panels and interviews (and conducted a few of the latter for the newsletter).

At present, Bonnie is a freelancer who writes marine related articles for scuba diving publications, including a monthly column for California Diving News, and illustrates them with her photographs. She also writes mystery novels and short stories.

Photographs of a few of the marine creatures Cinnamon Greene might encounter while diving off the California coast can be seen at www.bonniejcardone.com.

www.ingramcontent.com/pod-product-compliance
Lightning Source LLC
Chambersburg PA
CBHW030249130626
46549CB00002B/461